---------- ★ ----------

Frustrated, I pushed too hard against the slimy bottom and sent us into deep water again. We both went under, and I came up sputtering. Harry did, too, which I noted as I struggled, certain there'd be another shot now that I'd telegraphed our position. We were back in the shadow of the bank when it came. It sounded different from the others. Flatter. And I never heard the bullet strike water or stone.

That shot was the one I'd been waiting for, the sixth. After that there were only the sounds of traffic and the water slapping at the rocks.

Harry must have been counting, too, on some half-conscious level. "Revolver," he groaned. "Right again, God damn it."

---------- ★ ----------

"Mr. Faherty's tales are entertainment with a free flowing aorta."

—*The Midwest Book Review*

D0456511

Terence Faherty
Orion Rising

WORLDWIDE®

TORONTO • NEW YORK • LONDON
AMSTERDAM • PARIS • SYDNEY • HAMBURG
STOCKHOLM • ATHENS • TOKYO • MILAN
MADRID • WARSAW • BUDAPEST • AUCKLAND

ORION RISING

A Worldwide Mystery/February 2001

First published by St. Martin's Press, Incorporated.

ISBN 0-373-26374-0

Printed in U.S.A.

For Liza Cody and Michael Z. Lewin

PROLOGUE

Duchet's Heart

CAROL VANDERGALIEN had pert breasts.

I'd often read that description of breasts in paperback books, but I'd never really understood it until I met Carol. I looked the word up afterward and found that it meant "saucily free and forward." That described Carol in general, a daughter of north Jersey money who was working for the Middlesex County Historical Society as a way to pass the time. I was working there as a way of keeping body and soul together. Despite that difference, and a total lack of pertness on my part, Carol and I got on fine, which was fortunate as we were often given dirty, thankless jobs to do together.

We were working on one such job—sorting through unlabeled boxes in the basement of the society's townhouse—early on a Wednesday evening. We'd stretched the job beyond our normal quitting time because Carol had no symphony benefit or charity auction to attend that night and I had nothing to do that was half as interesting as sitting near a beautiful woman who laughed easily.

As a bonus, we'd discovered murders, a whole carton of them. They were the forgotten donation of a man named Roy Perkins, whose unpublished dissertation, "New Jersey Murder Pamphlets of the Nineteenth Century"—carefully typed in 1954—was the first thing we'd found in the box.

Carol paraphrased the paper for me, sitting on the basement steps with her elegant legs crossed, reading by the light of a naked bulb. "Listen to this. These brochures were popular souvenirs of famous murder cases. They were sold all over New Jersey and even in Philadelphia and New York, sometimes to benefit the victim's family, sometimes to benefit the murderer's family. The murderer's family? Oh, it says they were often sold at the hanging to cover funeral expenses. Some of them were a last claim of innocence on the part of the condemned. Most were confessions. The confessions sold better."

They always do, I thought. I was sorting through the pamphlets themselves, browned and crumbling, varying in size from tabloid to vest pocket. So far, I'd found "The Horrible Death of Amos Byrne, of the Merchants Bank of Boonton," "The Trial and Hanging of Zacheus Koster," and "The True History of the Murder on the Morris Canal Boat *Bridge Smasher.*"

Carol was reading further. "The railroads actually added special trains on the day of a hanging to accommodate the sightseers. Sightseers for an execution. Do you believe that?"

"Yes," I said. "I've been to a Jets game."

Carol smirked and read on. "The bodies of the hanged were given over for dissection. Sometimes souvenirs were made from the bones and the tanned skin. Yuck. They made stuff out of the skin. Pocketbooks even. That would take a lot of skin."

"They used to call wallets pocketbooks," I said, somewhat distracted. I'd found a booklet with a particularly gruesome cover, its centerpiece a bloody ax.

Carol set the dissertation aside and took the pamphlet from my hand. "The Crime of Pierre Duchet," she read. A moment later she was giving me a play-by-play.

"This happened in 1839, right here in Middlesex

County. A well-to-do doctor and his family took in a French immigrant, Pierre Duchet, as a laborer. One night after they'd gone to bed, Duchet murdered them all—doctor, wife and two kids—with an ax no less, for a few dollars in silver. Then instead of running, he got drunk.

"The kitchen girl, Polly Rees—our heroine—managed to get away and raise the alarm. The sheriff found Duchet asleep, covered in blood, a few silver dollars in his pockets and an empty brandy bottle next to him."

"How had Polly—our heroine—managed to get away?"

"She said Duchet spared her because she gave him extra treats with his dinner. And because he was sweet on her."

"The sex angle," I said. "You have to have that."

"Duchet claimed he couldn't remember anything that happened that night. Not too surprising after a bottle of brandy. His hanging was so well attended, they had to call out the local militia."

"The perfect murder," I said.

"Perfect? They hanged him."

"They hanged an innocent man," I corrected to tease her.

"Who did it, then?"

"Polly Rees, of course. The Nancy Drew of 1839. She slipped Duchet something at dinnertime to make him sleep. She was always giving him treats, remember? She probably used laudanum, from the doctor's supply. That was a big painkiller back then, opium diluted with brandy. She mixed it with a tankard of straight brandy, and good night Pierre. Then she chopped up the family, sprinkled Duchet with their blood or killed a chicken over him, and left him with the ax and a prop bottle. She traded her bloody nightclothes for clean ones, after washing herself in the old millstream by the light of the silvery moon. Then she was off to see the sheriff.''

"Why? What was her motive?''

"Motive. She did it for the money. The doctor was known to be well off, but they only found a few dollars on Duchet. Polly stashed the rest with her bloody clothes. Plus she hated her job. Plus Duchet wasn't sweet on her, she was sweet on him. Only he rejected her, so she framed him.''

Long before I'd finished, Carol was scanning the last pages of the pamphlet, looking for some rebuttal to my improvisation. What she found made her gasp.

She looked up, as frightened by me, it seemed, as by what she'd found. She dropped the booklet, muttered something about the time, and headed up the stairs.

I picked up the pamphlet and opened it to the last page. Attached to it was a piece of leather cut in the shape of a heart, but dried and shrunken. Beneath it was written, "Tanned skin of the murderer Pierre Duchet, obtained from Anne Willis, great-granddaughter of Polly Rees. Found among Rees's possessions after her death in 1871.'' It was signed Roy Perkins and dated 1952.

Just then Carol reached the top of the basement stairs. Forgetfully, perhaps, she switched off the lights.

ONE

"YOU REALLY OUGHT TO get a life, Owen."

Harry Ohlman had made the crack an hour ago, when he'd picked me up at the apartment I was renting in downtown New Brunswick. While he'd been standing in the apartment's living room, to be more specific, kicking at the newspapers that were keeping the carpet safe from dust.

"I've had one, thanks," I'd said.

At the time, it had seemed like comeback enough. Now, as we crossed the glittering Hudson on the Tappan Zee Bridge, a crossing I'd made often but never without the feeling that the river's true name was Rubicon, I wished I'd said something else. Something different. It wasn't the quality of the line I'd used that bothered me. No better one had suggested itself since. I was haunted by the fear that the claim I'd made to Harry simply wasn't true.

It was March 1995. We were driving from New Jersey to Boston, Massachusetts. To Boston College, our shared alma mater. Ostensibly we were going so Harry could oversee the audit of some accounts belonging to the alumni organization he headed up, Friends of the Eagle. In that scenario, I was along as relief driver or maybe just comic relief. In reality, we were making the drive on a crisp clear Sunday because a man named James Courtney Murray had recently been found shot to death in the office of his small accounting firm.

Murray had been the treasurer of Friends of the Eagle,

a coincidence that had inspired our cover story. It was certainly a coincidence. No one believed that Murray's volunteer work for the college had anything to do with his murder. No one believed his own work as a CPA had, for that matter. His killer had eliminated the need for speculation by leaving an old newspaper clipping on Murray's body, a clipping that described the brutal rape and beating of a nurse named Francine Knaff in March 1969 near Cleveland Circle, not far from the Boston College campus.

So I had more important things to think about than a stray insult of Harry's. But still, as the New York exits on the interstate gave way to Connecticut exits, I dwelt on the words "get a life," perhaps because they were easier to think about than James Courtney Murray.

It occurred to me that I might have done better at the apartment if I'd tossed Harry's words back at him. A widower married to a law firm he hated, Harry was a candidate for a little life enrichment himself. True, he was raising a teenage daughter, Amanda, or, as it sometimes seemed to me, being raised by her. And he was always involved with a woman, sometimes very involved. More than one had been sent his way by Amanda, a born matchmaker. But none of her schemes had worked out in the end. Harry always balked at the final fence, as his daughter, a veteran rider, had once put it. Although I knew perfectly well why he balked, I asked him about his latest failure now. As a payback, you might say. The latest in our long exchange of paybacks.

"What's happening with Lisa, the investment counselor?"

Harry swung the Lexus around a Suburban that was itself smacking the speed limit in the teeth. "Her name is Lena, and she's an investment banker. I'd explain the difference to you, if I thought you were really interested."

"I'm interested in how you two are doing."

"We're not."

I glanced over at Harry to see how I was doing, to see whether I'd made an impression. His face was a little red, but then it tended to be red, especially his broad straight nose and his cheeks, which waxed or waned with his weight. They were waning today, which fit with what Amanda had told me: Lena was an exercise nut who worked Harry hard. He wasn't thin and never would be— the big sedan's driver's seat was pushed back to the stops—but he'd sweated off much of the paunch he'd been lugging around since the eighties.

I checked the skin of his scalp, plainly visible through the remains of his dark hair, and decided I could safely push him a little further. "That's too bad. I was hoping she was the one."

"I bet you were," Harry said. "If I didn't know you so well, Owen, I'd think you were trying to free Mary up for some rendezvous in the afterlife."

So much for the reliability of Harry's epidermis. Mary was his wife, dead now for almost ten years. Dead but not forgotten by either of us. She was the reason Harry couldn't commit himself to another woman. My relationship with Mary was also ongoing, but less well defined.

Harry's mention of the afterlife would have sounded equally vague to an eavesdropper, had there been one around. Actually, it was very much to the point, an example of the kind of shorthand old friends use, an economical reference to a singular failure in my past: my unsuccessful attempt to become a priest. I couldn't be counting on some fleecy heaven where I might yet steal Mary away from Harry, not me, not Owen Keane.

I could have countered by saying there's a big difference between believing and hoping, as big as between waking and dreaming. I could have just said touché. I didn't say anything.

"We should be talking about Murray," Harry said. "You read the clippings I sent you."

It wasn't a question, but I answered it anyway. "I read them."

Harry must not have believed me. He started in on a summation of the case. He'd taken off his topcoat and sports jacket back in New Brunswick, but he still wore his gloves. They were thin and tight on his large hands, driving gloves in fact if not exactly in style. Harry tapped the steering wheel in a regular rhythm with his right hand as he spoke.

"Murray was working late a week ago Monday. Two weeks ago tomorrow. He was alone, as he always was in the office unless a client came by. His secretary quit a year ago to get married, and he never replaced her. Probably he couldn't afford to replace her. His business had never done very well.

"That wasn't in the paper," Harry added, in case I was anxious on the point. "I picked that up working with him on the Friends of the Eagle deal. I tried to get some kind of salary set up for him, tried to make him a staff member and not a volunteer, but he wouldn't hear of it. Too much self-respect."

That might have been another poke at me, a man who had supped more than once at the Ohlman trough. Or it might just have been Harry being sensitive and insensitive in the same breath. I didn't trouble myself to find out.

"Murray was staying late to meet a new client. Or someone he thought was a new client. He had an appointment noted on his desk calendar for seven that evening. All he'd written next to the time was 'Mr. Knaff.' There were no Knaffs in Murray's files, so it wasn't an established relationship. The police are figuring the killer used the promise of new business to keep Murray at his desk late, when there'd be less risk of someone in a neighboring office hearing the shots. They're still checking on the name, but it's likely to be a phony, a reference to Francine Knaff that Murray may or may not have picked up on.''

Harry changed lanes again and then said, ''I don't know whether you or I would have picked up on it, for that matter. Not after twenty-six years. And we have better reason to remember that name than Murray did.''

I was looking out the window. The stretch of highway we were on had been cut through an established neighborhood, laying bare a dizzying succession of backyards. I saw swing sets, tree forts, still-winterized swimming pools, scrap heaps hidden behind little sheds. Hidden from everyone but me. I thought of pictures I'd seen of bombed buildings, one wall gone, every room as open as a dollhouse's to the view of the world.

''When Murray didn't make it home by ten,'' Harry continued, ''his wife, Rita, started calling his office. I guess she also called a bar or two where he'd been known to stop after work. Finally, she got hold of the private security company that patrolled the little complex where Murray rented his office. One of their men found his body. He'd been shot six times at close range.''

My silence finally got to Harry. ''Are you listening, Owen?''

''Murray was shot with a revolver at close range,'' I said, without looking away from the scenery.

''I didn't mention a revolver. Neither did the police.''

"Almost every revolver holds six shots. Almost every semiautomatic holds more than six. The killer fired until his gun was empty. That's what you'd do if you were avenging a woman who'd been beaten to death. Or pretending to avenge one."

"I liked it better when you were daydreaming."

HARRY'S SARCASTIC permission for me to daydream might have triggered the memory. It had been waiting in the wings of my consciousness, crowded there with dozens of others, each watching for an opening ever since the news of Murray's death had reached me. I'd resisted them all until now. In a way, I still resisted, since the vision that took the place of the blurry Connecticut landscape had nothing to do with Murray or even 1969.

It was close, though. 1968. The fall of sixty-eight. Our freshman year at Boston College. Mine and Harry's and Mary's. I couldn't place the month. October? November? It was raining. I could see the rain on Commonwealth Avenue's black pavement, see it pooling in depressions in the granite curbing, each micropuddle reflecting the streetlights, making the stretch of curb where I stood look like gold-bearing ore. I could smell the rain, feel it pasting my hair—my shoulder-length hair—to my forehead and ears.

I was waiting under a tree that still had most of its leaves. I could hear them passing the raindrops to one another before depositing them on me. Beyond the trees on the other side of the avenue was Boston College, much of it out of sight below the crest of the hill atop which Commonwealth ran. I couldn't see Gasson Hall's great horned owl of a tower through the trees and the gloom, but I heard its clock strike nine.

Mary Fitzgerald was late. We'd agreed to meet opposite the main entrance to the campus at eight-thirty to wait for the Oldsmobile Bandit, as the television stations had dubbed the man who was robbing female hitchhikers around the greater Boston area. We were going to do more than wait for him. We were going to trap him.

I thought I'd worked out enough of a pattern in the bandit's crimes to make trapping him possible. He only struck on weeknights, usually late in the week, Thursday being his favorite day. He also liked bad weather, perhaps because it increased the number of hitchhikers, not that there was ever a shortage around Boston. He picked up lone women, almost always between nine and eleven o'clock. Picked them up, drove them a few blocks, robbed them, and let them go. His nickname came from the car he always drove, a metallic green two-door Oldsmobile whose license plate was always obscured by mud. The car seemed to be more memorable than the man, who was only described as white and slender and blond-haired.

The Oldsmobile Bandit worked the college campuses, maybe on the theory that hitchhikers enrolled in expensive schools might actually have a little money. He'd most recently struck at Boston University and Northwestern. He hadn't hit Boston College since early September. I had a feeling he was due back.

So I'd talked Mary, a coed from my apartment building dorm, a coed I was slightly more than friends with, into helping me catch the bandit. My clever plan was to wait on likely nights in likely spots for him to come along. Mary would hitchhike, and I would hide nearby, ready to step out whenever a car stopped. It was a ruse couples often used to snag a ride, although we weren't planning to get into any cars that night. I just wanted a look at the driver and his grimy license plate. Toward that end, I carried a flashlight tucked up the sleeve of my now sodden windbreaker.

I was tempted to take the flashlight out when I saw a figure coming toward me, climbing the hill from the trolley stop opposite St. Ignatius Church. It was the direction from which Mary should have been coming, but this wasn't Mary, wasn't a woman. I didn't relax until I recognized my roommate, Harry, and then I didn't relax much. There was nothing that reassuring about his expression or his greeting.

"She's not coming, Owen. I bumped into Mary just now on her way out of the dorm. She told me all about this dumb-ass scheme of yours. I told her I'd come instead."

"It won't work with you," I said. For one thing, Harry had a moustache, a heavy one whose ends grew well below the corners of his mouth.

"It won't work period," Harry said. "What the hell are you using for brains? Why would you bait a trap for a creep with a girl you know? With any girl?"

"He's never hurt anyone."

"He's never been threatened by anyone. And your bandit's not the only shithead working this city. It's stupid for any girl to be hitchhiking alone."

"That's why I'm here," I said. I started to explain the whole setup to him then, the parts Mary must have left out. Harry cut me off.

"You? You were going to protect her? Let me show you something."

He swung a lazy left at me. I blocked it easily with my right arm, aided by the flashlight splint in my sleeve. But the left was only a feint. With his right hand, Harry pushed against my chest. Somehow, he'd gotten his right foot hooked behind my left one. Though he hadn't pushed me hard, I went down that way, striking my head against the tree trunk behind me and shattering the flashlight's lens against the stone curb.

"That's how much help you'd be to Mary if you ever got her in a dangerous situation," Harry said. "Damn little."

He held his hand out to me. "Come on. Let's go home."

TWO

IT WAS STILL LIGHT when Harry, the Lexus, and I arrived at the outskirts of Boston, but we didn't stop at the Boston College campus in Chestnut Hill. There was no point in stopping on a Sunday, when the offices were closed. At least not in the opinion of Harry, a frequent visitor to the campus. I'd been looking forward to seeing the place again, but I had to content myself with brief glimpses of Bapst Library and St. Mary's Hall while Harry drove Commonwealth as though it were an extension of the Mass. Turnpike. He didn't glance over at the spot where he'd sat me down in the mud so many years before. Probably he didn't even remember it. He'd won so many more important victories since.

After he'd triumphed in law school and I'd snuck away from the seminary, we'd stayed out of each other's way for five years or so. Then I accepted a research job with his family's law firm in New York City. The job didn't work out—to put it very mildly—but it reestablished our relationship. When Mary was killed by a drunk driver some years later, it might have finished Harry and me by severing the only link we'd ever acknowledged. Instead, Mary's death somehow made my friendship with Harry a permanent thing.

Harry's life went off-road when his wife was taken from him. He tried to become a painter and failed, perhaps for the first time. That misstep could have been our new link, our true replacement for Mary. Failure was the theme of my résumé. I'd never held an important job or any job for very long. They interfered with my real career, the one that had alternately irritated and fascinated Harry for almost thirty years: the compulsive pursuit of mysteries.

Harry stopped, grudgingly, for a red light at Lake Street. Though we hadn't spoken for miles, he and I were thinking of the same thing, as often happened. In this case, it was my career.

"You haven't been with that county historical society very long, Owen. How were you able to get time off?"

"It was easy," I said. "I just left my resignation on their answering machine."

"Very funny," Harry replied, convinced I was joking. A second later, he wasn't convinced at all, but the light turned green, distracting him.

We were close to our destination by then, the hotel Harry had booked for us, the Chestnut Hill Dominion. There hadn't been a hotel on its site—the east side of Commonwealth Avenue at the South Street light—when I had last wandered by. I remembered red brick apartment buildings with no style or grace but with a beautiful view, standing as they had above the Chestnut Hill Reservoir.

Those apartments were gone now, I assumed because they'd been judged less valuable than the rocky hill they'd occupied. In their place was a tower of shiny granite panels and smoked glass. It wasn't much of a tower, only ten stories, but it dominated the old middle-class neighborhood. Harry pulled into its jug-handle drive, leaning forward in his seat so he could gaze up at the building.

"What do you think, Owen? Pretty amazing, isn't it? The college built this place. Not literally, of course. But the college's business made it possible, keeps it going.

Try to book a room here on a football weekend. You can't.''

He made it sound as though I'd been banned personally, at least on football weekends. I pictured a flashing message on the hotel's reservation computer: NO OWEN KEANES. But I only pictured it briefly. Harry was pulling to a stop, and we were being surrounded by Dominion employees, smiling young men whose burgundy uniforms were set off with gold piping. Burgundy and gold were the colors of Boston College, not coincidentally.

We disappointed most of this onslaught, since we only had two bags between us. I let Harry oversee their removal from the trunk, while I worked at not gawking at my surroundings. Just before the Lexus was whisked away, I remembered my trench coat, which I'd thrown on the backseat.

When I reached for the sedan's door handle, Harry said, ''You won't need it, Owen.'' I thought he was giving me a weather forecast, and I started to argue. Then I noticed that he was now wearing his own topcoat and carrying a second one over his arm.

''A present,'' he said, holding it out to me. And then, quickly, ''From your niece.''

The niece he meant was Amanda, who had called me uncle on and off ever since she could talk. Harry had never approved of the indulgence. That he was pretending to now told me he was slipping me more than a wardrobe upgrade.

''She thought it was time to give that trench coat of yours a rest. It's for your birthday, a little early.''

He was close to mentioning Christmas, too, as I'd still made no move to take the coat. He tossed it to me on his way to the hotel's revolving door. I stood there examining my present. Its material had an almost silky feel and was a medium gray in color. Amanda might have been trying to match my hair when she'd picked it out, if in fact she'd had anything to do with it. The coat was lighter than my old one, but that wasn't surprising, as it lacked a belt, shoulder straps, and all but a minimalist's idea of buttons.

I started after Harry. When the doorman, a wizened thirty-year-old, looked askance at me, I flashed the gray coat like a gold card. He nodded gravely and waved me inside.

Summer was waiting for me beyond the revolving door, summer in a tropical rain forest. It was warm and humid and the sound of a waterfall was drowning out all the incidental noises of the lobby. The sound wasn't piped in, either. The centerpiece of the space was a real waterfall, built of realistic-looking rock and rising as high as the mezzanine. This outcropping had plants sprouting from every likely crevice and, in the pool at its base, golden fish. I looked around for burgundy ones, but didn't see any.

By the time I found the reception desk, which was in a quiet cave behind the waterfall, Harry had already checked us in. We were down to one bellhop by then, but he'd acquired a chromium cart for the bags. He drove it one-handed, which enabled him also to pilot the elevator up to the tenth floor and to unlock the doors of our suite.

While this Renaissance man and Harry sorted out the two bedrooms, I examined the space that divided them, a combination living room, kitchenette, and bar, done in creams and grays. The wall opposite the entryway was almost entirely glass. The view was the reservoir, but the height of the tower spoiled it, making the large lake with its dark stone border seem no more than a pond, an outdoor equivalent of the lobby's captive waterfall. There were tiny figures jogging along the gravel path that circled the reservoir, and that surprised me. Before I could ask the bellhop about it, Harry addressed me.

"What do you think, Owen? A lot nicer than the first place we shared in Boston."

Nicer than the place where I currently lived, I thought, unsure whether Harry had omitted that comparison out of sympathy or embarrassment.

He was waving me over to a sofa that had its back to the suite's front door. "You might want to see this. It could come in handy."

The "it" was a computer the size of a laptop, mounted on a sofa table between twin brass lamps. As I watched, the bellhop, who looked to me to be a junior high school truant, switched on the little box. A greetings screen came up, listing Mr. Harold Ohlman Jr. and Mr. Owen Keane.

"You can check your bill at any time using this screen," the kid was saying as he tapped the keyboard. "This one is for express checkout. The room service menu is displayed on this screen. This one lets you see your messages. You each have a separate message area, a pigeonhole we call them. You can enter messages for each other or for other hotel guests using this screen, either from this unit or from any of the units in the lobby. Your pigeonhole is password-protected, so it's completely secure."

"Nice to know something is these days," Harry said as he handed our instructor his tip.

I wandered into the bedroom on the right. My bag was on the quilted queen-size bed, looking seriously underdressed. The gray color scheme was repeated in the bedroom, but the cream accents of the living room had given way to lavender, most notably in the wallpaper, which featured huge flowers I couldn't place.

I walked into the matching bath and switched on the light. The mirror over the sink was lit like a Broadway star's. I could see every hair I'd missed when I'd shaved that morning, every line on my well-lined face. The expression my reflection wore was quizzical, but there was nothing new in that. Nothing new either about the navy blazer I'd chosen for the drive. But it looked different somehow, with its home-sewn buttons and shiny lapels. Out of place.

I still carried the gray raincoat. I slipped it on, hoping to finesse the sensitive mirror as I had the doorman. It fit very nicely.

"Going somewhere?" Harry asked from just outside the door.

"Thought I'd take a walk," I said, off the top of my head.

"Good idea. We can work up an appetite for dinner."

THREE

ON OUR WAY DOWN in the elevator, I asked Harry about the reservoir joggers. "I heard they'd padlocked the trail years ago."

"They did," Harry said. "Too many muggings and worse. They reopened it when the Dominion was built. For the use of the hotel's guests. All the other gates are still locked. The path is lit at night now, and there are security cameras."

"Have they scented the water?"

"Not yet," Harry said without smiling. "Were you wanting to walk around the reservoir?"

"No," I said.

"Me either."

Without conferring further, we left the hotel and turned right along Commonwealth Avenue, heading away from the campus. At Chestnut Hill Avenue, we made another right, skirting the eastern bank of the reservoir until we came to Beacon Street.

The area was known as Cleveland Circle for no reason I could ever work out. There wasn't a traffic circle there, not as they were defined in the rest of the civilized world. The intersection of Chestnut Hill and Beacon and a couple of smaller roads was more of an asphalt no-man's-land, an ongoing game of chicken with an occasional streetcar thrown in for bonus points. Harry and I stood taking in the noise and confusion for a moment. Then we turned to climb a narrow side street named Sutherland.

We didn't climb far. Two Sutherland Road was our

unstated destination. It was an apartment building, like every other building on the block. And it was about the same vintage as the others, seventy years old, give or take a decade. But it was by far the smallest. The narrowest, I should say, since at five stories it was of average height. I'd always imagined that the land had once belonged to a holdout house, the last single dwelling on a street that had been taken over by apartments. Finally the house had been torn down and replaced by the biggest building that could be squeezed onto its lot, a red brick and worn limestone one that still had some characteristics of a house, including an off-center front porch and a bay window repeated in each story of the facade.

"Home again," Harry said. It was all either of us needed to say.

WAS IT THE SAME night that Harry saved Mary Fitzgerald from bandits and amateur detectives? It seemed so to me as I drifted back, but that might have been foreshortening caused by distance or some editing for dramatic effect courtesy of my unreliable memory.

It had certainly been an evening in the fall of 1968. An evening when Harry and I returned to Two Sutherland together. I was sure of that much. We climbed the stairs to the third floor that night and found a crisis in progress.

We were residents in the building in the first place because of a crisis: a shortage of campus housing. Boston College had overdosed on freshmen that year, seduced by a buyer's market born of the Vietnam War and draft exemptions. The college's solution was to buy four old apartment buildings and to cram five or six freshmen into each two-or three-bedroom apartment, with floors of women alternating with floors of men. At least that had been the practice in three of the four buildings that shared a little courtyard cum air shaft at Cleveland Circle. The fourth, Two Sutherland, hadn't fit the pattern. Each of its five floors had been a single three-bedroom apartment in the building's heyday. The college installed two freshmen in each of the bedrooms and two each in the former living rooms and dining rooms. The ten residents of each floor shared a kitchen and a bathroom, whose shower drain was perpetually clogged with hair rosettes.

Harry and I had lucked out on our room assignment. The front rooms, the living and dining rooms, were bigger and had better views, but the room we had drawn, on the courtyard end of the building, was almost two rooms, as it included a glassed-in back porch, unheated but just large enough for both our desks. Our room was also moderately isolated, being separated from the other bedrooms by the bathroom and the kitchen, which stood opposite one another across the hallway that ended at our door.

The crisis meeting that Harry and I blundered into that night was being held in the kitchen of our floor, the third floor. Most of the eight other men from three were jammed in there, along with representatives of the first floor and the fifth. None of the women of Two Sutherland, who resided on the second and fourth floors, had been invited.

We actually heard the meeting before we saw the overflow crowd in the hallway, heard the topic—almost shouted—as we stepped onto the third floor landing: "Fucking fags."

"What the hell?" Harry said. He pushed his way through the gallery in the hall and into the doorway of the kitchen. I followed, slipping through the gap Harry created a second before it disappeared behind him.

"Ohlman, good," the guy who had held the floor since we'd come within earshot said. "Keane, too? Good."

I could see him over Harry's shoulder, a big broken-nosed guy from upstate New York with the phonetically challenging name of Tregnab. All I knew about him was that he'd tried to make the college's football team as a walk-on and failed and that he had a phony ID that kept the dorm supplied with beer.

"I was just telling the guys we had a situation," Tregnab said.

"Which is what?" Harry asked.

"O'Brien was down at Copley Square today and saw Steven Stapella putting up a poster for the Greater Boston Homophile League. That means fucking queer, homophile."

"I know what the word means," Harry said.

"Stapella saw O'Brien and took off through the crowd. But it was him all right. Which means we got one of them living right here with us."

"'Angels and ministers of grace defend us!'" The mocking quotation had come from a thin guy squeezed in between the refrigerator and the sink. James Courtney Murray. He'd picked his location strategically; he had an open can of Budweiser in his hand, and there was an empty on the counter next to him.

James Courtney Murray. One of the few residents of the dorm with a genuine Boston accent. One of the better accents, too, as he was a graduate of the Boston Latin School. Dark-featured with a beak of a nose that was set high on his thin face, or made to seem high by a slightly weak chin and a long neck. His large blue eyes, also weak, gazed at Tregnab through wire rims. Gazed innocently, as though Murray was as surprised as anyone that he'd opened his mouth.

"Shut up, Barrymore," Tregnab said.

Murray raised his beer can, accepting the order or the compliment or both.

Harry broke in. "What business is it of ours what poster Stapella was putting up?"

He'd cut to the only question there was to discuss, the one that Tregnab and the others hadn't gotten around to discussing. I was already used to that habit of Harry's. It surprised Tregnab, but he found his feet quickly. "This is *our* dorm is what business it is of *ours*. We've got a right to say whether we share it with a homo."

"He's not your roommate," Harry pointed out.

"Yours either," Tregnab shot back. "How would you like it if he was? Would you trade Keane for him?"

Trade me for Stapella? Given our recent disagreement over my crime-fighting techniques, I expected Harry to jump at the deal. I wouldn't have blamed him for saying yes just to shut Tregnab up. Harry didn't say anything, at least not fast enough.

The answer came from the other kitchen door, the one that led to the back stairway: "I would."

I had to stand on my toes to see the new speaker, Alan Avery, and then I could only see the smallest part of him through the packed room. One deep-set eye, cut across by dark brown hair and deadly serious.

I've described the Cleveland Circle residents as freshmen, but we had two types of exception. There were the resident assistants assigned to each building, harried graduate students who seemed ancient to me. Our own RA, a recent Irish immigrant named Foley, usually found other places to be, as he had tonight. There was also a handful of transfer students sprinkled here and there throughout the four buildings. Avery was one of these. He was a junior, which would have been enough to make him an unelected leader of the dorm. But he had other, better recommendations. One was the rumor that he had left his previous school under a cloud, getting into Boston College only because of his family's money. His second shining quality was his sexual appetite. He had a different woman in his room nearly every weekend, to the admiration of all of us, even Foley, who pretended not to know.

"I'm sure Pete would be happy to swap with Steve," Avery said, referring to his freshman roommate, who slept on the floor in other people's rooms whenever Avery entertained. That got a laugh from the crowd, albeit an incomplete one, as Tregnab refused to join in.

"Of course," Avery continued, "we haven't heard yet whether Steve's roommate is as scared of him as some of you seem to be. Who is it, anyway?"

He asked so casually that I was sure he already knew and that he was playing his trump card. Stapella's roommate was a casualty in the making named Ellison, an economics major who had discovered marijuana during his first week in Boston and had been stoned ever since. Harry jokingly referred to Ellison as morally constipated because of the answer he invariably gave to any question.

Ellison gave his pet answer now when Avery asked him whether he minded having Stapella as a roommate. He looked up from his seat at the kitchenette's little table and said, "I don't give a shit."

"There you go," Avery said smoothly. "If Ellison is broad-minded I don't see why the rest of us shouldn't be. None of us is lily white. I know I'm not. I say we leave the guy alone."

"So do I," Harry said.

"Me, too," Murray and I chimed in, stepping on each other's moment of moral independence.

Tregnab was ready to tally the opposing votes, but Avery didn't give up the floor. "Anyone who thinks he's here not to meet different kinds of people should have stayed home. I like a mix myself. Even with the occasional weirdo."

He must have been looking right at Tregnab, judging from the way the latter reddened when the crowd laughed again. I strained to see Avery through the shifting bodies, but he was already gone, his "Goodnight, kiddies," coming down to us from the stairwell.

It would be nice to record that Avery's stand and Harry's had carried the day, that Stapella had been treated well or just plain ignored. But that didn't happen. I never was exactly sure what did happen, what form the harassment took. But within a month Stapella had packed up and left in the middle of the night. It was several days before Ellison sobered up enough to notice.

FOUR

THE NEXT MORNING Harry and I left the Dominion Hotel early and joined the lava flow of traffic creeping down Commonwealth Avenue toward the city proper. We stuck with the avenue the whole long way, right up until it ended at the Public Gardens. The last few blocks were ones I'd never driven before, a sylvan run between brownstones and a statued esplanade. The interlude created the false sense that the city became more civilized the nearer you approached to its heart, more parklike and spacious.

That impression faded when we made the right onto Arlington and was gone completely by the time we'd turned left onto Boylston, fighting unsmiling pedestrians who were—on this bright Monday—a bigger problem than the other cars. When we crossed Tremont at the corner of the Boston Common, the street's name jogged a memory, a fairly recent one for a change.

"I thought I'd read that the new police station is on Tremont," I said.

"It is," Harry replied. "Tremont and Ruggles, way back by Northeastern's campus. The cop we're going to see works downtown. Special liaison to the mayor's office. Relax and enjoy the scenery."

There wasn't much scenery left to enjoy. And the foot traffic, which intensified as we entered the oldest part of the city and the streets narrowed, made relaxing impossible. Harry took Washington Street to Court and then backtracked a block on Tremont to a parking garage that was across the street from King's Chapel. We became troublesome pedestrians ourselves then, following Tremont until it turned into Cambridge and crossing that to Government Center and City Hall, a poured concrete building whose top floors were bigger than the bottom ones. The locals called it the Aztec Tomb because it vaguely resembled an inverted Aztec pyramid.

The wind was coming off the harbor with a vengeance. We leaned into it as we climbed the last set of plaza stairs, Harry holding on to the flat woolen cap he wore to shelter his surviving hairs. On the last dash to the Tomb's revolving doors, we bent our heads down as though we were expecting a blessing.

Once inside, we followed signs for the Mayor's Office, then smaller ones for the Boston Police Department Liaison Office. The last sign, a very small one, identified the office of Lieutenant Harry Gilder. We'd been stopped several times along the way. At each hurdle, Harry had mentioned his name and his appointment and been cleared. I'd followed along in his wake, falling back easily into what was an old habit.

That Harry and Lieutenant Gilder shared first names was no coincidence. They were cousins, members of a prominent Boston family that took things like beating Christian names to death seriously. Neither man was a prominent member of the prominent family. Harry's own father had been banished to New York because the Ohlmans' Boston firm lacked an empty desk. Gilder, son of an Ohlman daughter who had married a politician, hadn't even gone into the family business, the law. He was in a related field, though. Whether Gilder had chosen that field for himself or been assigned it as a way of serving the greater Ohlman good, Harry hadn't told me.

I stood to one side as the Harrys greeted one another.

There wasn't much in the way of a family resemblance, as Harry took after his mother. Gilder, a head shorter than his cousin, looked a little like Harry's father, his features more delicate than Harry's and less open. These were topped off by a full head of reddish brown hair, which may have been a gift from the Gilder side of the family.

When he finished with Harry, the lieutenant shook my hand. While far from effusive, the greeting was among the friendliest I'd ever gotten from a policeman. "Just been reading about you," he said, gesturing toward some loose pages on his desktop as he walked around to his seat.

I couldn't read them from where I stood or from the chair Gilder waved me to, couldn't even identify the sheets beyond noting that they were bad photocopies. Perhaps copies of copies. Instead of straining my eyes, I looked around for family photos, a weakness of mine. I saw one near the corner of the desk where Harry sat. Though it was turned toward Gilder, I could just make out the smiling faces of four children.

"How's the audit coming?" the lieutenant asked Harry as he sat down. He didn't wink as he asked it, but he might as well have.

"It'll be tomorrow," Harry said. "And it will go fine."

"Don't be so sure. A guy who'll rape and beat up a woman isn't likely to be too particular about decimal points."

"Why are you so sure Murray was a rapist?" Harry asked. "Isn't it bad procedure to take his murderer's word for that?"

"We didn't," Gilder said. "We've seen enough cop shows to know that newspaper clipping could have been a blind. It was from the *Boston Globe,* by the way. There was a duplicate in our file on the Cleveland Circle murder.

"That's an interesting file." He tapped the photocopies on his desk. "I managed to get a copy of it, humble political flack though I am. You never told me you'd been a suspect in a murder case, Harry. That must have sent shivers through the family."

"It did," Harry said.

Gilder looked from Harry to me. "How did your folks take it?"

"I never told them."

"Surprised the college didn't. Guess they would have if you'd been sent up and they'd had to refund part of your tuition. I can't believe I didn't hear of it through the family grapevine. I was in high school at the time, but still. The Ohlmans are better at keeping secrets than I thought."

"It's a lot of what we do for a living," Harry said.

"Just the opposite of my job," Gilder replied. If he was issuing Harry a warning, it was a very subtle one. Too subtle to worry me.

"Are you saying you've confirmed that Murray was the Cleveland Circle rapist?" I asked.

"Yep. The DNA report just came in. As you may recall, there wasn't much physical evidence from the 1969 attack. I guess it rained pretty hard that night and hosed the crime scene down. A lot of what they had were some brown hairs that got caught in the victim's—Francine Knaff's—class ring. It was a ring from the nursing school she'd attended. That wasn't much of a lead in sixty-nine, but today even a single hair can tell you a lot. At least it can if you have a genetic sample from a suspect to compare it with.

"There are hair samples from both of you in our evidence file. Enough of yours to weave you a rug, Harry, which—no offense—you really could use. Almost as much of yours," he said to me, "in its original lustrous brown. Less of Murray's, but then we didn't need to use his old samples. We had his whole body on a slab.

"Anyway, it all checked out. The DNA from the murderer's hair sample matched Murray's, more or less."

"More or less?" Harry asked.

"Don't ask me to explain that DNA stuff. I don't pretend to understand it. Your DNA mutates over time, I'm told. Exposure to nuclear fallout or television or Big Macs with fries. Who knows? So you would expect there to be minor differences between Murray's DNA now and the sample Knaff ripped out of his scalp twenty-six years ago. But they were only very minor. The match was so good the odds against it being a coincidence was something like one in ten million. More than enough to clinch it, even if we didn't know of Murray's previous involvement in the case. James Courtney Murray was the Cleveland Circle rapist, no doubt about it."

He watched us for a minute or so. "You guys don't look very relieved. You get cleared of a murder every day or something?"

"That DNA test was done awfully quickly," Harry observed.

"Yes, it was. The laboratory just started using a new test, something faster it wanted to show off. The lab boys figured this case would be perfect for showing off, since Murray is dead, which means he'll never be tried for Knaff's murder, which means his lawyers will never hire any expert witnesses to drag in DNA contamination and other mumbo jumbo to cloud issue. All the lab will get when the results are made public, which will be soon, is a nice article in the Sunday paper."

"There's Murray's widow," Harry said. "She could hire lawyers and expert witnesses."

Gilder shrugged. "Why would she waste her money? From what I hear, she hasn't got it to waste."

"Why weren't DNA tests done prior to Murray's murder?" I asked.

Gilder squinted at me, the squint making his features even more ferretlike. I suspected he had glasses hidden away somewhere that he was too vain to wear. "Excuse me, Mr. Keane?"

"You had hair samples in the old file from the murderer and all the suspects. You could have compared them any time after DNA testing became available, any time during the past few years."

"Guess the detectives assigned to rifling cold-case files for ones that can be cleared up with the latest whizbang technology screwed up. Not that it would have mattered in this case, conviction-wise.

"In their defense, the cold-case squad has one hell of a lot of unsolved crimes to keep tabs on. Most times, the pressure to take another look at an old crime comes from the original investigating officers or the victim's family, which may explain why nothing was done in the Knaff case. The cops who worked it are all dead or retired down to Florida. And the victim never had much family. A lot of the investigating we've done since Murray's murder has been trying to trace living Knaffs."

"Where does the investigation stand?" Harry asked.

"I'm not assigned to the case," Gilder reminded him. "Hadn't even read up on it until Uncle Charles called to say you'd be stopping by. So my information is second-hand at best. But it seems they're stuck. That's the way it is with these things. They either break quickly or they tend not to break. I'm sure the investigating team would appreciate any information forwarded by any public-spirited citizens.''

He paused again, ending this time-out with another shrug. ''They're taking the killer at his word and treating Murray's death as a revenge hit for the murder of Francine Knaff. That's become almost a sure bet now that the DNA info is in. As I said before, there was always a chance that Murray's murder had nothing to do with Knaff's, that his killer simply knew about his connection to the old crime and was using it as a smoke screen. But now that we know for sure that Murray was Knaff's killer, the chance of that clipping being a screen gets much, much smaller. The shooter would had to have known that Murray was guilty of the sixty-nine crime or just lucked out, which is the kind of coincidence I find hard to believe. It would be like one of those made-for-TV thrillers that always make me want to get up and pace.

''Of course,'' he added after he'd worked the idea over, ''maybe Murray's killer didn't know he was guilty. Maybe he plans to bump off each of the half-dozen guys from your dorm who made the suspect list on the theory he'll get the rapist sooner or later. Maybe we should make those DNA results public before he strikes again.''

This time when Gilder paused it was for a laugh he didn't get. ''The problem is,'' he continued, ''we haven't been able to find many people who even remember Francine Knaff, never mind want to avenge her. The best our guys have done so far is a cousin who lives over in Springfield. I might be able to set up an interview with him if you're interested.''

''Thanks,'' Harry said. ''We'll think about it.''

The policeman took our lack of enthusiasm in stride. ''If Murray's killer used his own name to set up the appointment, it would be the only mistake he made that night. No one saw him arrive or leave. There were no unaccounted-for fingerprints.

"No shell casings. No loose hairs of any color wrapped around Murray's ring or anywhere else on his person. Did I mention that we'd be grateful for any help we can get on this one?"

Harry politely ignored the prod. "You intimated just now that you would have had trouble getting Murray convicted if you'd tested the samples in the sixty-nine evidence file prior to his murder. Why?"

I mentally gave Harry extra points for that question, a very discreet way of getting at the one thing Gilder could still tell us: Who had had access to that evidence?

The lieutenant waved a hand dismissively. "You know as well as I do that DNA evidence by itself is no sure sale to a jury. There's a bigger problem with the Cleveland Circle material. Let's just say it wouldn't meet our current standards for evidence integrity."

"Mice get in it?" Harry asked casually.

Gilder gave him a long look. "This isn't something I'd like to see quoted in a complaint filed by Murray's widow."

"You won't," Harry said.

"There may have been some irregularities involving the evidence file. The case file, too, though that's more of a venial sin. I've only heard rumors. It seems a local researcher, a professor at your old school, BC, was given a copy of the old case file. This particular researcher, Dr. Phyllis Garrity, is almost a cop herself. That is, she's a nationally recognized authority on rape and a consultant to our department. She asked to see the Cleveland Circle file for a book she's working on. One of the cops she'd helped in the past said okay. He shouldn't have, but he did.''

''Where does the evidence file come in?'' I asked. ''It's not kept with the paperwork file, is it?''

''No, it's kept in the evidence room. The rumor I've heard is that Garrity got a peek at that, too. I don't know the whole story, but I could find out.''

''I'd really appreciate it,'' Harry said.

''Anything for family. Call me in an hour. And that reminds me.''

He lifted the papers before him and retrieved a single index card. ''That woman you asked me to trace. Her most recent married name was Timony. She was killed in a one-car wreck in ninety-two. So much alcohol in her blood it was like blood in her alcohol. What's her connection with this?''

''No connection,'' Harry said. ''Just an old friend I wanted to look up. I'll call you in an hour.''

FIVE

WE HAD TIME to kill before the next appointment Harry had set up for us. We walked east past Faneuil Hall to the Quincy Market. The old sheds had been gentrified since our college days, turned into places for tourists to eat stir-fried food, buy T-shirts, and sip expensive coffee.

We were after coffee, as it happened, but Harry bypassed the cappuccino franchises in search of a greasy breakfast counter he remembered from the days when the market still sold fresh vegetables and fresher fish. We couldn't find the place or anyone who even remembered it. Harry glumly settled for Starbucks, compensating himself with a sweet roll from an adjoining bakery. We sat under the market's central dome on stools that looked and felt like giant toy blocks.

"So somebody rigged that DNA test," Harry said after a time.

"Yes," I said.

"Somebody who had access to the old evidence file and maybe to Murray's corpse, if the hairs that were substituted for the rapist's were taken from Murray's dead body."

"They weren't," I said. "Those DNA mutations your cousin mentioned wouldn't have shown up if hair from Murray's corpse had been added to the file. Whoever did the switch worked with the file alone. They took a little from the sample identified as James Murray, suspect, and substituted it for the hairs recovered from Francine Knaff."

Harry tore off a piece of the sweet roll and dunked it in his coffee. "Agreed," he said. "But who? Someone connected with the police? This researcher professor?" He showed that he'd been thinking back on our college days himself by adding, "I'd ask why, too, but you'd probably quote Sherlock Holmes at me, something about the danger of theorizing before you have all the facts."

We were all of us doomed to theorize before we had all the facts, I would have said if I'd been in the mood for philosophy. The big paneled doors of the rotunda had been propped open to admit the chilly air. My stool gave me a view of the cobblestone plaza beyond. I watched a young office worker stride past, her open coat sailing behind her like a cape. She was kept warm, perhaps, by the smile she was smiling to herself. I smiled, too, noting that skirts had risen sometime while my mind had been otherwise occupied.

"Focus, Owen," Harry said, without smiling. "We have to work this out. Before the DNA test results are made public."

"Agreed," I said.

AT TEN O'CLOCK we were standing inside the entrance to the Boston Public Library, the modern entrance in the modern wing, which looked like an airline terminal slammed down next to the old classical wing by mistake. We were between the street doors and the security checkpoint—another airport touch—a row of metal detectors with wood paneling applied to soften their looks.

Harry was fascinated by the gateways. "I wonder if they're to keep people from sneaking books out or guns in?"

He walked over to an information desk while I day-

dreamed about afternoons I'd killed exploring the library.
When Harry came back, I asked, "So which are they?"

He looked at me blankly.

"The gates. Are they for guns or books?"

"Oh. I didn't ask that. I wanted to know about back
issues of the *Boston Globe*. The killer had to get that old
clipping somewhere. It wasn't from here, though; the library's old issues are on microfilm."

Before I could claim to have known that already, a
woman addressed us. "Mr. Ohlman? Mr. Keane? I'm
Rita Murray. Thank you for agreeing to see me here. I'm
sorry I couldn't have you come to my house or my office.
Most of my coworkers have stopped asking me about
Jimmy's death every ten minutes. I don't want to get
them wound up again."

"We understand," Harry said. "Would you like to sit
down somewhere?"

"Not in here," Murray said quickly. "There are
benches by the church."

"Afraid Owen and I will get the librarians wound
up?" It was Harry being charming. Luckily, that was
how Murray chose to take it.

She smiled, wanly. "No. I'd like to smoke. It's an
outdoor activity these days."

By "church" Murray meant Trinity Church, the old
tourist attraction that always looked to me like an upper-
class Victorian's idea of a mosque. The church was in
the next block, beyond a little park. On the way there I
had time to examine Murray, as none of us was in the
mood for small talk. She was younger than her late husband, and, consequently, than Harry and I. Thirty-five or
thirty-six to our forty-four and change. She was an attractive woman, though part of that was a certain damaged quality, a hollowness in her cheeks and a darkness

around her eyes. That is, her fragility would have been an attraction to a certain type of man, one drawn to women in peril. A wide spectrum of men would have been drawn to Murray physically, to her blond hair, her long legs, and her body, which wasn't at all fragile.

She wore a business suit with a jacket almost as long as her skirt and with material as shiny in spots as my blue blazer. I wondered if Harry was considering making her the present of a topcoat. He was certainly thinking hard about something as he conducted his own furtive examination.

We found an open bench between young maple trees that were all orange buds and silver branches. Harry lit Murray's cigarette and a cigar for himself with a wind-proof lighter.

"Thank you for seeing us," he said. "As I told you on the phone, we're here to oversee the audit of the accounts your husband maintained for Friends of the Eagle. We wanted to represent Jim at the audit. We were friends of his."

"He spoke of you," Murray said to Harry. She looked at me less confidently. Most people did.

"I lived on the same floor as your husband when we were freshmen," I said. "I'm afraid we didn't stay in touch."

"The building on Sutherland Road?"

Harry answered for me. "We were all freshmen together."

"So you know about the… You know what happened there."

"Yes," Harry said.

"You can believe it, then," she said. "It's real for you. It isn't real for me, the old murder. It seems like something out of a movie or a book. That's exactly what it's like, reading in the paper that Jimmy was a murderer. It's like turning on the television and seeing him in some old movie. Unreal. My doctor says it's just been too much. All of that coming on top of Jimmy's own death. He says it will all sink in later. I hope it never does."

"Your husband never mentioned the Cleveland Circle attack to you?" I asked.

"No. I've thought a lot about that, wondering if that wasn't a sign that he really was involved."

"It would be just as likely for an innocent man not to mention it," Harry said. "To have forgotten it, I mean."

He wanted to say more, but he checked himself without benefit of a warning glance from me. Murray warned him herself with a dangerous look of hope. "The police are still investigating," he said. "They might find out he was killed for a completely different reason."

"What different reason?" Murray asked, getting to the crux of our agenda. "Jimmy didn't have any enemies. He didn't have any money. He wasn't doing the books for the mob. Or if he was, they weren't paying him very well. He didn't covet his neighbor's goods or his neighbor's wife. That was Jimmy's only bad habit, not coveting. Being satisfied. Settling. His only bad habit besides beer. He's the only one he ever really hurt, and beer's what he hurt himself with."

"Why would he hurt himself with anything?" I asked.

"For not being the big success he'd talked about being when we were young. We met while I was still in high school. He was a brand-new CPA. Too old for me to be seeing, but I didn't listen to any of that advice. He had a little ambition then, but it didn't last. By the time Melanie, our daughter, was born, it was all gone. He was content with the world then, or would have been if I'd laid off him.

"I was harder on him than I should have been. Over money. Over letting me and Melanie down. I can't remember now why I thought any of that was so important."

"Jim often spoke of Melanie," Harry said. "How is she doing?"

"Not well," Murray said. Like her late husband, she had a Boston accent, but in her case it wasn't one to make a Kennedy groupie weak in the knees. South Boston, I thought. "She hasn't been herself for the past few years. Hasn't been the little girl I knew. She's a teenager—an unhappy teenager, even before this happened. Melanie doesn't like herself much at the moment, and she's trying to make the world agree with her.

"She was hard on Jimmy, too, I think because I always was. He was an easy target, someone to blame for everything she didn't like about herself. They'd always been so close, the two of them, when she was a little girl. She hurt Jimmy a lot when she turned away.

"If all of that weren't enough to make Melanie miserable now, she has to deal with the possibility that her father was a murderer and a rapist. I complain about the people in my office, their empty sympathy and their whispering, the conversations that end when I enter the room. But that's nothing compared with what Melanie's gone through at school. The only thing worse than a teenager is a building full of teenagers.

"I'm not being the help to her I should be. I never do the right thing anymore."

She ran out of steam then. She might have cried, but I sensed she was also out of tears. Harry, whose right hand had been hovering near hers through the whole speech, leaned toward her. "I know a little about what you're facing," he said. "I've a daughter myself. My wife died in 1986."

"How old is your daughter, Mr. Ohlman?"

"Call me Harry. Amanda is fourteen."

"Fourteen," Murray mused. "That was when the bad times really started for Melanie. She's eighteen now. Should be the happiest year of her life. I'm sure it was my happiest. She should be picking a college, a life. She won't even talk about any of that. She won't talk about anything but a rape that happened almost thirty years ago. Not the murder, either. Just the rape. That's what's preying on her mind. The idea of her father as a rapist."

"Melanie is the reason you wouldn't see us at your home?" I asked.

"Yes," Murray said. "Sorry. It's silly to hope she'll forget it any faster if she doesn't meet you, but silly hopes like that are a lot of what I have left."

She ground out her cigarette on the cement arm of the bench and held the stub in her cupped hand. "Let me know how the audit goes," she said as she stood.

Harry stood, too. "We're here to do more than referee the audit. I mean, if there's more we can do, we will. If there's anything you think of, anything you need, anything you'd like to talk about, we'll be staying at the Chestnut Hill Dominion."

To demonstrate his usefulness, he took the cigarette filter from her hand.

"Thanks," she said, smiling with a little more life this time.

We watched her until she disappeared in the crowd crossing Clarendon Street. Then Harry said, "We caused this, Owen. We're responsible for what that woman and her daughter are going through."

"I know," I said.

SIX

WHEN WE WERE BACK in the Lexus and rolling, Harry
opened a lid on the center armrest and tapped a number
into the phone hidden there. I kept my eyes on the traffic,
but I would have done as well to have shut them and
prayed. Harry didn't pick up the handset, so the sound
of the other phone ringing filled the car, courtesy of a
hidden speaker.

"Gilder," the answering voice said.

Harry addressed a tiny microphone located near his
visor. "It's Harry. What do you have for me?"

"Are you calling on a car phone? I'd rather use a land
line for this. Hell, I'd really rather use a confessional."

"If you're paranoid," Harry said, "we'll speak in
code. How recently had this Dr. G been by to see the
evidence file?"

"She didn't have to visit it. It was in her possession
at the time of, ah, M's death."

"I'm talking about the evidence file, not the old paperwork file."

"So am I."

"Are you running a police department or a lending
library?" Harry asked, looking across at me but keeping
his tone casual.

"Damned if I know. The detective involved had consulted with Garrity—damn I mean, Dr. G—on a number
of rape cases. He didn't think there'd be any harm in
letting her see the old case file on Cleveland Circle. It
was bending the rules, but I would have bent that one

myself. But Dr. G also wanted some postmortem photos that happened to be in the evidence room. Our coopera-tive detective signed out the evidence file and handed it to a junior officer to sort out for Dr. G. The kid passed her everything by mistake. We had to get it back from her so we could find out what we knew, departmentally speaking.

"Needless to say, those two haven't done their careers any good. But the file was intact, so there was no real harm done."

He was asking Harry a question. Harry answered it with "Thanks."

Gilder's sigh came over the airwaves clearly. "You're going to make dinner at Uncle Charlie's tonight, right? Everyone's looking forward to seeing you."

"I'll be there."

"Is your friend the accountant coming? Or is he going to be busy with his abacus?"

Harry grinned at me. "I haven't asked Owen yet. And he's not an accountant. He just looks like one."

"What is he, then?"

"A gentleman sleuth."

"No shit? I didn't think there were any of those, out-side of books. I'm sorry I didn't take a picture when I had him here. See you tonight."

WE HAD A quick lunch at the hotel and then walked to Boston College. Climbed to it, I should say, since the campus occupied a series of hills above the reservoir. We could have stuck with Commonwealth all the way up, keeping the campus to our left and entering by the main drive, the one that ended at the pillar on which the col-lege's golden eagle perched. But Harry wanted to give me a guided tour of some of the more recent construction.

We went in through a gate by the football field, whose stands had grown enormously, it seemed to me. I asked Harry if they had made the field bigger, too, but he didn't answer me. Instead he pointed out the student athletic center, whose roof resembled a Bedouin tent village, and the new residence buildings on the hill beyond it, where there had been nothing but trees in our day. We climbed the hill on an open concrete staircase, joining the two-way student traffic. I scanned the opposite lane for faces I knew, by which I mean echoes of faces I'd known, and saw them everywhere. Even the hair styles and clothes looked oddly anachronistic.

"Have we stumbled into some kind of sixties festival?" I asked Harry's back as we climbed.

"You should check in with Amanda more often," he said. "She'd keep you in touch. The sixties are in again. We should have driven up here in that old Volkswagen of yours."

"With flowers in our hair," I added sarcastically. We wouldn't have stood out much more if we'd had them, two middle-aged men being passed on the stairs like overloaded semis on a mountain turnpike.

We stepped off the top of the staircase onto more familiar ground, in the shadow of a building where I'd had a biology lab. "Higgins Hall," Harry said without troubling to look at the name chiseled into the stone above the door. All the buildings were stone here and the same stone, a golden-brown limestone. The architecture varied according to the age of the hall. The oldest were in a pseudoclerical gothic style with steep gable roofs and vestigial spires. The newest were complicated cube collections with flat roofs and no ornamentation. In between were hybrids, the whole collection united by the golden stone. I wondered, as I'd wondered in 1968, whether the college had a private quarry somewhere that was only worked when classroom space got tight.

There were kids everywhere. Kids who were the same as the ones I remembered, the way the water in a river is always the same though always new. Harry caught that sense, too, and responded musically, softly whistling the opening bars of "San Francisco," the old Scott McKenzie anthem, a song I might have put in his head with my joke about flowers in our hair. However he'd come up with the it, the tune was the perfect background music for our march into the past. So perfect, I could almost hear the tambourine.

Between bouts of whistling, Harry rattled off the names of the buildings like a tour guide. Cushing, Fulton, Devlin, Lydenburg, and on and on. I might have done as well myself given a little time or a little scotch. This middle earth portion of the campus was that much like home.

Beyond it things changed again. I remembered a stretch of level, open land, a little breather before the campus resumed its climb, this time into the dormitory ghetto. The intervening quad, called the dust bowl, had been an informal gathering place, part park, part sports field, part open market. Now most of it had been swallowed up by another building, a big windowless fortress of a place.

"The new theater," I said. "The Nimoy Center."

"How did you guess that?" Harry asked. "It looks more like a jail from the outside."

That was appropriate, as I'd once been arrested on the lawn where the building now stood. Harry might have been alluding to that with his jail crack. Instead of asking him, I said, "You described it to me once."

We circled the theater counterclockwise and crossed

College Road. Our destination was a little white house, one of a row of houses the college had bought up along the western edge of the campus. This particular house was now called Burke Hall, and it was the home of the Office of Alumni Oversight and Coordination, or the OAOC, as Harry always called it. Friends of the Eagle was one of the alumni fundraising groups sanctioned by the OAOC. Harry's team was dusting the competition, to judge by the greeting he got when we entered the office.

We were shown into a little conference room whose table size suggested it had once been the home's dining room. Harry and I sat and waited, the table between us. The walls were paneled and hung with photographs of aged priests. Jesuit priests, given the college's affiliation. The Jesuits had been thin on the ground when Harry and I had been students. I wondered how many were kept for appearances' sake these days.

The director of the OAOC was no Jesuit. She was a plump, somewhat harried woman in her fifties with thin hair that faithfully followed the contours of her pear-shaped head. Her body was also pear-shaped, what I could see of it above the table and around the bulging folder of papers she carried across her chest. In her other hand was an insulated mug decorated with the college seal. I could hear ice cubes tapping as she bent to kiss Harry, half out of his seat, on the cheek. She nodded to me before taking the chair at the head of the table. By then Harry had introduced us and the director, Koie Mustafa, had offered us coffee or ice water, raising her mug to illustrate the second option.

"We're all in shock," she said, still wearing the file folder as a breastplate. "I don't think there's a person in this office who didn't smile every time James Murray came through the door. I can't think of him as a murderer, can you?''

"No," Harry said.

"But it's just as hard to think of him as a murder victim, and we know he was. So I suppose everything else is true, too."

"I suppose."

"You were right to request an audit." Here she finally laid her paper bundle on the table. "Do you suppose there'll be discrepancies?''

"No," Harry said. "But it's best to be safe. In case anyone questions us later."

"Exactly," Mustafa agreed. "I have to confess that we weren't expecting you today. The auditors nominated by the college won't be making their preliminary report until tomorrow afternoon."

Harry lifted his hand from the tabletop and let it drop back onto its reflection. "We just thought we'd touch base today. Let you know we were here."

The "we" reminded Mustafa that Harry hadn't come alone. She addressed me, smiling. "So, Mr. Keane, are you a Friend of the Eagle?''

"More like a third cousin," Harry quipped.

"But you are an alumnus."

"Yes," I said.

"I'll look you up on our computer and check your giving record," Mustafa said playfully. "I'm sure you've been generous."

"Please don't bother," I said, afraid she'd turn up unpaid library fines and worse.

"Owen did have a question to ask you," Harry put in, all but kicking me under the table. "I told him you were an authority on the faculty."

He'd actually called her a particularly well-connected

gossip hound, which I was tempted to tell her, just to drop him a peg.

"I do take an interest in our teachers," the director said. "They're such an intriguing group."

"I'm interested in a BC professor named Garrity. Phyllis Garrity."

"I don't know much about her," Mustafa said, her expression adding that the little she knew she didn't like. "The woman who teaches about rape. Psychology department, of course. Let me see. She's a bit of a firebrand, I've heard. A radical, at least by Boston College standards. I'm afraid that's all I know, except that she's been here forever.

"Her husband now, he's someone we've all heard of."

"Have we?" I prompted before Harry could take a swipe at me with his tasseled loafer.

"The college features him regularly in its promotional mailings. We had him in our alumni magazine just this year. I'm sure you saw the article on him. Wayne Woodson? He's been asked to serve on the Pulitzer Prize committee for literature."

She rose in her chair and called toward the open conference room door. "Imogene! Bring me the January issue of the *Alumni Report*. There's one in reception."

Imogene found two copies of the glossy magazine, which, at Mustafa's direction, she handed to Harry and me. I flipped through mine until I came to the story on the Pulitzer appointment. It was accompanied by a color photo of the leading light himself, a man of fifty something who had large protruding blue eyes, a regal nose, tightly curled gray hair, and a neatly trimmed beard, which was slightly more brown than gray, almost as brown as his tangled eyebrows. Woodson's expression was friendly, but the overall effect of the pose, of the way he seemed to be leaning away from the camera actually, was something altogether different. Imperious was the word that came to mind.

I started to scan the article that went with the photo, noting that Woodson had recently celebrated his thirtieth year with the college. Garrity was briefly mentioned, along with the couple's daughter, Bergen, an editorial assistant with an unnamed publishing house in New York. Then Mustafa told me to take the copy with me, making further speed-reading unnecessary. She and Harry returned to the subject of the audit, Harry agreeing to revisit the OAOC offices the next day at four.

"What will you be doing to occupy yourself until then?" the director asked, openly curious.

"Just poking around," Harry said. He took his parting peck on the cheek like a man.

SEVEN

OUR MENTAL TELEPATHY ACT was still working; Harry asked Imogene the receptionist for directions to the psychology department as we left the OAOC office. We hurried there—the second floor of McGuinn Hall—the hurry being instinctive but totally justified, as it turned out. Dr. Garrity was locking the door to her office as we walked up, bending over the job intently, like a miser locking a vault.

"Sorry," she said after she admitted being the woman we were after. "I'm on my way to a class. Was there something I could help you with in two seconds or less?"

We'd discussed our approach to her over lunch. I would have improvised something completely different now if I'd been alone, due to nerves or a subconscious need to screw up. Harry calmly stuck to the plan.

"We're friends of James Courtney Murray," he began. "We're here to help with an audit of some alumni accounts he maintained for the college. We heard you were writing a book on the Cleveland Circle rape, the one Murray's accused of committing."

"Heard from whom?" Garrity asked, every bit as matter-of-fact. She was almost short, a slightly stooped back squandering a little of the height she had. Her dark hair was definitely short—it had been shingled in back like a marine recruit's—which emphasized the angular, fleshless quality of her face, a face like windswept stone.

"A friend on the Boston police force," Harry replied. "I hope your friend knows his own business better than he knows mine. It happens that I'm writing a book on the psychology of rape. The Francine Knaff rape is just one of twenty case studies I'm considering. Now if you'll excuse me, Mr....?"

"Ohlman. Harold Ohlman."

Garrity raised the book she was carrying until it covered her heart, unconsciously duplicating Koie Mustafa's defensive posture. "You were a freshman here in 1969," she said.

Harry nodded.

Her dark eyes clicked to me, the movement that rapid and mechanical. I said, "Owen Keane. Also class of seventy-two."

Ohlman and Keane, two names from the Cleveland Circle file. Garrity was suitably impressed. "Well," she said. "Shall we walk while we talk? I'm late already."

She signed a log on the department secretary's desk and led us down a crowded stairwell, setting a pace slightly faster than jogging. Harry had a bad leg. He hadn't favored it through all the walking and climbing we'd done that day, but he began to now as he struggled to keep up.

"Tell me," Garrity said as we exited McGuinn. "Have you come forward to help me with my research?"

"Perhaps we can help each other," Harry said. "We're having trouble accepting that James Murray could have committed such a terrible crime."

"Maybe you won't have to. Maybe he didn't do it."

"I'm afraid there's no longer any hope of that," Harry replied from a step behind her right shoulder, as close to abreast of her as he could manage without breaking into a trot. "The police have done a DNA comparison using the hairs recovered in sixty-nine."

"I see," Garrity said. From my station on her left, I

was better placed than Harry to read her expression. She seemed sincerely sorry to hear the news.

"Did James Murray help you?" I asked.

"I beg your pardon?"

"Was he a source for your research?"

"No. I never met the man. He was just a name in the file to me. I had no idea he was still living in Boston until he turned up dead in the *Globe*."

We arrived at Garrity's destination, Fulton Hall. At the door was a traffic jam of students, each as late as the professor. Harry was able to catch up and even shoulder his way ahead a little, helping to clear Garrity's path— or appearing to—as he stepped up his examination.

"You were researching the old case long before Murray was shot."

"Of course," Garrity said.

"So the resolution of the case is a fortunate coincidence?"

"It would be fortunate if I were trying to write a bestseller. The publicity would be a godsend. As I am writing a scholarly text for a limited audience, my only gain is whatever additional knowledge the investigation uncovers."

"Would you mind telling us why you selected that particular crime for your book? It was all but forgotten, even by the police."

"Perhaps it bothers me that a crime that heinous could be forgotten," the doctor said.

"Is that the reason?" I asked from my new post directly behind her.

"No. As it happens, the Knaff case was what first drew my attention to rape. I was a graduate student and teaching assistant here at Boston in 1969, when you two gentlemen were living down at Cleveland Circle. I wanted to understand how such a horrible crime could take place in what I then considered to be an enlightened, loving era. Being a scholar, I naturally turned to books for my answer. I found the work that had been done on the psychology of rape to be pitifully small. Much of what existed was flatly wrongheaded, being based on the antiquated patriarchal notion that rape is a sexual act, when in fact it's an act of violence.''

She finally noticed that Harry had subtly shifted from blocker to roadblock. She stepped around him and into the first-floor hallway, which was emptying rapidly. There she again hit warp speed. Her lecture continued, accompanied by the sound of our six shoes on the linoleum floor.

''As it turned out, what I was really discovering with that research was my life's work. I've been trying to expand our knowledge of the rapist's mind ever since.''

''Never getting very far from Cleveland Circle,'' I observed.

Garrity stopped short, requiring Harry to sidestep like a dancer to avoid knocking her down. She looked at me as though I were a student who had mouthed back. That was what I felt like, anyway, inspired by the sights and sounds of Fulton.

''Staying at Boston wasn't my choice, Mr. Keane. There were many schools that would have been more receptive to my work, especially in the early years. But I was a married graduate student. The man I'd married was a Boston College professor who refused to ever be anything else. So here I am.''

It said a lot about Wayne Woodson, I thought, that he'd been able to keep this woman at BC all these years against her will.

''Perhaps you gentlemen would like to sit in on my

lecture," she offered as she resumed her march. "If you're really interested in your classmate's actions, it might be of some help. In exchange for which, you might let the students question you about how it felt to be suspected of rape."

She stopped at an open doorway. I could see then why it had been necessary for her to leave the comfort of McGuinn. The room beyond the door was a small amphitheater, and it was very nearly full. "Do you remember how it felt?" she asked.

"Not very clearly," Harry said, speaking for himself. It was all I could do to keep the memories at bay. "So I don't think we'd be much of an addition to your lecture. And I don't think your students would be very interested in the other questions we came to ask you, regarding your handling of the Cleveland Circle evidence file."

Garrity considered Harry for a moment. Then she turned to stick her head into the classroom. The students had settled themselves as soon as she'd appeared in the doorway, which confirmed what I'd already guessed about Garrity's classroom personality. "Begin reviewing chapter eleven," she said. "We'll discuss it shortly."

She shut the door. "What questions did you have, Mr. Ohlman?"

"How were you able to obtain the police evidence file?"

"By accident. I asked for all the information on the case including photographs from the postmortem, if possible. You're not the only ones with friends on the police force. What I received was everything they had, including the physical evidence, such as it was. I was quite surprised."

"Too surprised to send it back?" Harry asked.

Garrity never blinked. "My plan was to send it all

back, when I'd finished with it. I suppose I should have acknowledged their mistake and returned everything but the case file and the postmortem photos immediately.''

"The rest of the evidence file wasn't of any use to you?" I asked.

"What use would it have been? I'm a psychologist, not a detective. Is that what you became, Mr. Keane? A detective?"

"Excuse me?"

"What I was principally after were the interviews the police had conducted with the likely suspects. I was looking, as you gentlemen are now, for understanding, for an insight. Your interview was the most interesting, Mr. Keane. The police didn't know what to make of you. I'm surprised they didn't arrest you for that reason alone. But then, you're very...nonthreatening in person.''

"Thank you," I said.

"You actually tried to interest them in some theories you had about someone who was robbing coeds from a car. Do you remember that? And you were very vague about your alibi for the night of the attack. 'Walking in the rain.' More of a song title than an alibi. The police were certain you were holding something back. And the officer who interviewed you made a two-word marginal note that intrigued me: 'religious issues.' He didn't include an explanation. I was disappointed.''

I was, too, but I didn't admit it.

It was Harry's turn next. "They didn't think much of your alibi either, Mr. Ohlman. What was it? Trying to get drunk in a bar where no one subsequently remembered you? What did you become, by the way, a musician or a painter? You were undecided as a freshman.''

Harry proved to be harder to rattle than I was. "We accept that you've had access to the background checks and interviews the police conducted in 1969," he said. "Although it's harder to understand how violating our privacy advanced your research. You can't have believed that more than one of the men whose private information you were rummaging through was the rapist. And you couldn't know which one it was."

"A lawyer," Garrity said, as unruffled now as Harry. "That would be my guess for you. You're right, of course. I couldn't know which of you was the rapist. But maybe it didn't matter to me. Maybe I'm one of those feminists who sees every man as a rape waiting to happen. Maybe the fascination for me was reading about six clean-cut sons of the middle class, knowing that I couldn't pick the rapist out.

"Or maybe I wanted to play detective myself, but not with the physical evidence, which is, after all, someone else's province. Maybe I wanted to get into the mind of the rapist, to identify him using what I've learned about a rapist's thoughts and motives."

"He was also a murderer," Harry said. "You've never mentioned that."

"Murder isn't my specialty. In any case, the murder was incidental to the rape. Francine Knaff was a victim of what we call anger rape. The rapist beat her in an uncontrollable rage; the photographs I obtained of Knaff's corpse confirmed that very vividly. Her attacker intended to hurt her badly, but probably not to kill her."

"Were you able to identify the rapist based on your reading of the old interviews?" I asked.

"No. James Murray fooled me, just as he fooled the police in 1969. But then he was an actor, wasn't he? At least he was in college. I gather from the articles I've read since his murder that he didn't follow that ambition up. Why not, I wonder?"

"He didn't want it enough," Harry said, falling back on Rita Murray's assessment of her husband.

"Maybe the rape poisoned it for him," Garrity said. "It happens. A rapist who goes unpunished by society sometimes punishes himself. Sometimes by arranging for a lifetime of failure."

She was speaking of Murray but looking at me. "Where did you keep the files?" I asked.

"In the office I have in my home. Locked in my office safe when I wasn't using them. That was a condition I agreed to when I obtained them."

"Is it possible anyone else handled the files?" Harry asked.

"Quite impossible," Garrity said. "So you gentlemen can relax. Your confidential information will remain confidential." She opened the classroom door without turning away from us. "Now if you'll excuse me, I'm short-changing a roomful of paying customers. If you care to chat again in the future, you might make an appointment through my secretary."

EIGHT

WE WERE ONLY a few steps outside Fulton when Harry reached for his cigar case. He'd struggled for years to give up cigarettes, only to fall for the cigar craze on the say-so of a glossy magazine with role models like Arnold Schwarzenegger on its cover. Harry only smoked illegal Cubans, which he obtained from a shop in Canada, the identifying cigar bands being mailed to him under a separate cover. I liked to think that the bands were counterfeit and the shop was slipping Harry cigars rolled in Perth Amboy. It made me more patient with his sniffing and cutting and lighting ritual.

When the latest worship service was over, Harry said, "Interesting that Garrity assumed we'd be getting in touch with her again. And that she didn't congratulate us on being cleared of the Knaff murder, the way my cousin Harry did."

"She couldn't," I said. "Not sincerely. She knows that Murray was innocent. So she has to suspect that you or I could be guilty. In fact, since we've shown up on her doorstep with awkward questions about her handling of the evidence file, she has every right to suspect us of having guilty knowledge."

We were standing on a thin patch of grass on one of the busiest corners of the campus, but we felt comfortable discussing the case. Apart from an occasional look of disapproval directed at Harry's cigar, the student traffic was treating us like a pair of alumni lampposts.

"She has every right to suspect us," Harry repeated,

but he sounded unsure. He began to run through the logic of it to double-check me. "We're assuming that Garrity knows that Murray was innocent. We're assuming that because someone switched the hair samples in the evidence file to make it appear that Murray was the rapist. Only someone who knew he was not would bother. But how do we know it was Garrity?"

"We don't," I said. "We're guessing." Harry didn't like that bald truth, so I covered it slightly. "The only people who handled the file were the two Boston policemen and Garrity. Unless one of those cops is Francine Knaff's long-lost nephew, we're left with Garrity. We have her own testimony to the effect that she and she alone handled the files once they reached her. We may not be justified in accepting that, however, since we also know she's lied to us."

"When?"

"When she claimed to have no interest in the physical evidence. It was pure chance she got her hands on that, but I think she made the most of the chance." I had an inspiration then, but I stated it as a fully formed idea. "I think she commissioned a DNA test of her own and it exonerated Murray."

"Whoa, Owen. You said yourself she isn't sure who really was the rapist, that she suspects one of us. How could she not be sure if she conducted DNA tests? Her inside information has to come from somewhere else. She has to have some personal knowledge of the crime from 1969."

"How could she? How could she be involved? Do you remember her?"

"No," Harry said.

"Me either. I'm still betting on a DNA test. But it has

to be that she only tested Murray's DNA against the sixty-nine rapist's."

"So she wasn't interested in who the rapist was?" Harry asked, suitably incredulous. "She was only interested in whether or not it was Murray? Why?"

A young woman passed us. Dozens had since we'd been standing there, but this one made me work at breathing. She had long brown hair spread out across the shoulders of a green jacket, worn open, despite what had become a very cool afternoon. A green jacket, bell-bottom jeans, and desert boots. I only caught a glimpse of her face as she turned her head away from a cloud of cigar smoke, which made the deception possible, made it possible for me to convince myself for a nanosecond that she was someone I knew.

Harry's "why" was still on hold. "We can't know why yet," I said. "We can't reach that far."

Harry smoked and thought while I watched the girl in the green jacket disappear around the corner of Fulton. "If Garrity only tested Murray's sample," he finally said, "she has to have some special interest in Murray. So she has to be lying about not knowing him."

"Agreed," I said.

"Even so, Owen. If your reasoning is right, if Garrity knew that Murray was innocent, then she has to have a motive for killing him that has nothing to do with the Cleveland Circle attack. As my cousin Harry says, that requires the kind of coincidence that makes you want to get up and pace."

"Not a coincidence," I said. "A connection we don't understand yet. Besides, who said Garrity killed Murray?"

"*You* said she switched the hair samples."

"I said I'm guessing she did. Even if I'm guessing

right, it doesn't make her the killer. She could have made the switch to protect someone else, someone who sincerely believed that Murray was the rapist.''

I was guessing again, but there was something to it. I could tell by Harry's reaction. His cigar had rolled to the center of his mouth and was drooping dangerously. As I watched, the long tip of ash he'd been nursing dropped onto his shoe. ''Too much?'' I asked.

''No. That kind of leap is exactly why I wanted you along. But it's enough for now. Let's be sure of our footing before we climb any higher. Let's have a real investigation for once and not a butterfly hunt.''

''Pile on another metaphor,'' I said. ''Make it an even dozen.''

''I'm only saying we should check what we can check, try to stay as close as we can to what we can prove.''

I was always open to a new approach. ''What can we prove so far?''

Harry strode off purposefully. ''We can find the lab Garrity used for her DNA test, if it exists.''

Halfway back to McGuinn there was a pay phone on a pole stuck in the sidewalk. Harry commandeered it and punched in a number.

''This is Harry Ohlman. I'm staying in Dominion suite three. Right. Could you send a courtesy car to the Beacon Street gate of the Boston College campus?'' He put his hand over the mouthpiece and addressed me. ''I don't want to be limping around my family reunion tonight. I can be soaking my leg while I'm arranging for the local branch of the family law firm to find that DNA lab.''

''You're not...'' I began and stopped when the phone addressed him.

''The corner of Beacon and Lawrence,'' Harry told it.

"Five minutes? Great. Goodbye. What were you asking, Owen?"

"Why you're not using the police."

"My cousin can only divide his loyalty so far. Better to save him until we really need him."

We walked to the end of the service road to await the pickup. Harry's pickup, as I'd decided to extend my walk. He was anticipating my desertion. Maybe even counting on it.

"I take it you won't be coming tonight," he said.

"Better not. I might make one of my leaps and end up in the punchbowl."

He dropped his cigar into the gutter. "Just don't end up in a punchbowl somewhere else. Eat at the hotel, charge it to the room."

"Okay." We watched the traffic for a dozen cars or so. Then I said, "Do you know anyone in the registrar's office?"

"No, but I'm sure Koie Mustafa does. Why?"

"Call her while you're soaking your leg. Ask her to get us a copy of Murray's transcript."

"Using what as my justification?"

I couldn't imagine the worshipful Mustafa asking Harry for one. "Tell her you want to quash a rumor that Murray was a spy for Holy Cross."

"I'll think of something myself," Harry said.

The Dominion courtesy car, a Lincoln, arrived at the curb. Harry took it for granted that I wouldn't be joining him on its double-wide backseat. He even seemed to know where I was headed. "Don't get lost on Memory Lane," he said as he shut the door.

I REENTERED the campus and followed the route taken by the girl in the green jacket. I had no serious hope of finding her and no real interest in it. I was hoping instead to find the woman I'd mistaken her for. Mary Fitzgerald. An infinitely longer long shot.

This time I took the left-hand path around the theater building, skirting Carney Hall, where I'd had most of my classes in my major, English. Beyond it was McElroy, the student union. It marked the end of the flat ground that had once been the dust bowl. In fact, McElroy was set right into the next hill. You could enter it, as I did, on the ground level, the bookstore level, ascend a series of stairways, and exit the building on the cafeteria level, well up the slope.

I crossed the little plaza in front of McElroy, remembering that it had been the bus stop for the shuttle the college had run between the campus and Cleveland Circle. I'd often spoken to Mary there, when I'd been lucky enough to find her waiting. She'd lived on the floor below mine at Two Sutherland, but that had seemed too intimate a setting for our first conversations, which had been about Hemingway, whom Mary had considered overrated, and chess, about which I'd known only the basic moves. I'd regretted that when I found the game was a passion of hers.

From the plaza I climbed into the dormitory ghetto, a nickname only students who'd never seen a real ghetto could have invented for a wooded hillside crowded with red brick, slate-roofed dormitories, all identical but for their names and reputations. At what was roughly the center of the complex was an old mansion, O'Connell House, perhaps the original structure on the hillside, certainly the pattern for the brick and slate used everywhere else. At one time O'Connell had been the residence of one of the college's many deans, but by 1968 the noise from the surrounding dorms had driven out the last Jesuit.

After that the mansion had been used for receptions and banquets and little else.

There had been a dinner there on the evening in 1968 when Mary Fitzgerald and I had had our first date. I stood outside of O'Connell and thought back to that night. Background music for the reverie was provided by a nostalgic and hardy soul who had his dorm window open. I could faintly hear "In-a-Gadda-Da-Vida," a recording Harry had once played mercilessly.

IT HADN'T STARTED out as a date. We'd both been invited to a party in the lounge of one of the old dorms by a mutual friend, also an English major. It was a keg party and well out of hand when I arrived. Some problem with the keg tapper had beaten the best available minds. I stepped into booing and yelling that was louder than the music, and then Mary was at my side. Mary, tall and thin, her light brown hair spread out across her shoulders, the strands nearest her pale face curling from the communal heat and sweat. My eyes went right to the mole on her cheek that I'd told myself never to look at and then to her eyes, very blue and very serious.

"Thank God," she shouted in my ear. For a second I thought she was expecting me to fix the keg. Then she said, "Let's get out of here before the riot starts."

We walked out into the night, Mary's arm still wrapped around mine. Together we wandered the dorm ghetto, passing more than one party in meltdown. We talked about our families and found they had a lot in common, though the Fitzgeralds occupied the safer middle ground of the middle class. We discussed *Crime and Punishment,* a book we were reading for a freshman survey class. I teased her by maintaining that the hero of the novel was really Petrovitch, the detective. She tightened her grip on my arm—already so tight I couldn't get her breasts out of my mind—when a shower of stolen cafeteria plates, launched from a third-story window, shattered on the asphalt path behind us.

"We can never go back," I said. She laughed and didn't let me go.

At the end of one circuit, we found ourselves at O'Connell House. A party had been held there, too; it was a night of parties. The O'Connell example had been the most sophisticated yet, according to the evidence scattered along the courtyard wall: plastic drink glasses still wrapped in napkin coasters, hors d'oeuvre plates complete with uneaten cubes of cheese that were growing toothpicks with blooms of Easter basket grass, empty bottles of imported beer.

"Looks like we accepted the wrong invitation," Mary said. And then, when I started to lead her through an opening in the wall and onto a flagstone porch, "Where are you going?"

"I'm investigating," I said. "I'm an investigator."

"Of what?" Mary whispered. We were crossing the porch, heading for open French doors.

"Unturned stones," I said.

Beyond the doorway, a large room had been set up as a buffet. Long folding tables set end to end and covered in paper ran down the center of the otherwise unfurnished space. The lights were off. What we could see of the tables had been cleared of everything but stains and spills.

"Too bad," Mary whispered. "I'm hungry."

She regretted that admission when I slipped inside the house, motioning for her to keep quiet. I followed the table line into the darkness, attracted by an aroma and by a round shape I could just make out on the buffet's far end. It was a turkey, one side carved down to the bones, the other untouched.

"Owen!" Mary whispered.

"It's all right. We're both on the meal plan."

I took hold of the uncarved leg and yanked it free. Mary was already halfway to the French doors, but I almost beat her through them. I was leading again as we cleared the courtyard wall. We didn't stop running until we were far enough from the house to laugh safely. Then we laughed for a long time.

I offered Mary the first bite from the leg as we resumed our walk. She took what was, given her small, perfect mouth, an amazingly large bite. When she'd finished chewing the tough skin, she said, "There's your constellation, Owen. No, over there. Just over that tree. See the big rectangle? That's Orion. He pops up this time every year. Those three faint stars are his belt. I can't see his sword tonight."

"What makes him my constellation?" I asked, my mouth full.

"He's a hunter. Orion the Hunter."

"Owen the Hunter," I said, brandishing the turkey leg over my head. "Scourge of dead turkeys everywhere."

"Owen the Investigator," Mary amended, taking back the leg. "Overturner of stones."

NINE

I DIDN'T TAKE Harry's suggestion and eat dinner at the Dominion Hotel. Instead I walked down to Cleveland Circle, where I'd noticed a little Greek restaurant when Harry and I visited the night before. I'd remembered then that Mary and I had once eaten dinner in a Greek restaurant that had surely been in the same building, though it had had a different name: the Aegean Green. Now it was the Parthenon. The dimly lit storefront had been redecorated at least once since my dinner with Mary and was due again. I stayed anyway, drinking beer and eating spanakopita but getting no sense of that lost night.

Afterward I walked down Beacon to a neighborhood where I'd lived after I'd dropped out of the seminary, when it had looked for a time like I'd end up a prisoner of Boston, as Phyllis Garrity seemed to be. I visited the liquor store where I'd clerked, Nab's, but there was no one there I remembered or who remembered me. I was tempted by the shelves of dusty bottles, but I started back to the hotel without one.

I found someone waiting for me there, a young woman bundled up in an old pea jacket. She and the coat were in turn bundled in a leather armchair near the lobby goldfish pond. I saw her look across at the bell captain, saw him look at me and nod to her. Then she was digging her way out of the leather sleeping bag and hurrying to intercept me.

"Mr. Ohlman? Mr. Keane?" She was very pale from what I could see, though the lobby wasn't lit much better than the street I'd just quit. Pale with large blue eyes whose lids and lashes were painted darker than her dark straight hair. Her hair looked wet, and I wondered if she'd sat too close to the waterfall.

"Mr. Keane," I said.

"Mr. Keane, you don't know me. You talked to my mother today."

"She spoke of you, Melanie," I said, extending my hand. When she finally took it, I said, "Please, call me Owen. I'm surprised she told you about seeing us. She didn't want us to come to your house this morning, Harry Ohlman and me. We were both friends of your father's. Your mother was afraid we'd bother you. She said you've been having a bad time since your father's death."

"Did she?" Melanie asked. She seemed undecided over how to take Rita Murray's frankness. "Mother can be...overprotective."

I was equally undecided over what to do with her. I didn't want to take her into the hotel lounge or up to the suite. In the end, we stayed in the lobby. The chair she'd been using had a twin, which sat on the opposite side of a block of polished pink stone that supported a single crystal ashtray. Like Rita Murray, Melanie was a smoker. She drew a cigarette straight out of her pocket as we sat down. I pictured her lifting a few from Rita's pack on her way out of the house.

"Does your mother know you're here?"

"No. You don't have to tell her, do you?"

"She won't be worried?"

"Not this early. It isn't even eight o'clock."

I had to look at my watch before I'd accept that. After all my walking, it felt more like midnight.

"I want to talk to you. About my father."

"Okay."

I thought she'd start with the big question. She looked like the kind of person who asked the hard ones easily, who wore her mother down with them and scared her teachers. She started with a softball.

"What was he like when you knew him?"

"I liked him," I said. "He seemed pretty sophisticated to me. The way he always introduced himself using all three of his names. He didn't dress like any of the other kids either. Ten years later, when everybody was copying his style, they had a name for it: preppy. He dressed that way when the rest of us were trying to look like we'd just hitchhiked home from Woodstock. I don't know where he found the clothes. From some old-line men's store, I always imagined, where they could fit you out for anything from a wedding to an expedition up the Amazon. And he was always quoting Shakespeare."

"Shakespeare?"

"*Hamlet*. He'd gotten himself into a production of *Hamlet* almost as soon as we'd arrived that first year. The rehearsals lasted most of our first semester. At least it seems looking back that they did. He was always going off to a rehearsal. And quoting the speeches he'd heard."

"It's hard to picture him acting," Melanie said.

Phyllis Garrity had been fooled by the old reports into thinking of Murray as a would-be actor. Even Harry seemed to remember him as someone with a serious interest. I didn't see any harm in telling Melanie the truth.

"It was a girl. A woman, I should say. She was a sophomore or a junior. I can't remember which. A blond, I remember that. Your father saw her once and fell in love. That's how he got into the play. He saw her at some kind of activities festival for freshmen. All the campus organizations had booths, and she was sitting in one for this Shakespearean group. He signed up for *Hamlet* then and there. She was going to play Ophelia, I think. Your dad went to every rehearsal, even though he didn't have a line of his own. He memorized everyone else's part while he was trying to catch her eye.''

"Did he end up raping her?"

I'd been leaning forward in my chair, working too hard at selling the story. I settled back now, feeling as though the leather cushions were swallowing me. Hoping they would.

"Sorry," I said. "I should have picked another story. I just don't think of your father as a rapist."

"I can't think of him as anything else," Melanie said. She retreated into the depths of her own chair and took a long drag on the cigarette she'd been ignoring.

"Your mother told me the kids at your school have been making things hard for you."

"I don't need anyone's help for that. I only have to read the newspapers. You don't believe them, do you, the newspapers?"

"What do you mean?"

"You're not really here because of an audit."

I'd had the feeling when Harry had been spooning Rita Murray our story that she'd been doing more chewing than swallowing. "The audit's already underway."

"But it isn't really why you came to Boston. Are you here to find out who killed him? Why would you do that for a rapist? Why would anyone care who killed a rapist?"

"Like I said, I don't think of your father as a rapist."

If Harry had been handy, he would have stopped me by then, would have spoken the warning I was flashing myself: Don't get her hopes up.

"You're just trying to make me feel better."

If I was, I needed to work on my technique. She looked

even paler, if that was possible. Paler and more desperate.
I expected to see her heavy mascara running down her
cheeks at any moment.

"Would that be such a bad thing?"

"It would be a miracle."

She added her cigarette to the ones she'd previously
deposited in the crystal ashtray. Then she stood up.
"Would you mind if I came back to speak to you again?
Will you be here?"

"Only for a couple more days," I said. "But you're
welcome to come and talk. You might try the daytime."

"I'm not big on daylight. About my mother..."

"I won't mention seeing you."

She turned down my offer of a cab or company as far
as the trolley stop, shook my hand, and left.

MELANIE MURRAY'S small hand had been ice cold, and
I carried its chill with me, up into the suite. Once inside,
I checked the little message computer, looking for home-
work assignments from Harry. He hadn't left me any. I
checked his messages next. We'd agreed to use the same
password for our separate electronic pigeonholes: Murray. When I typed it in and pressed the return key, I saw
that Harry had one message, a voice mail, received at
eight o'clock, when I'd been saying good-bye to Melanie.
The message log gave the phone number of the caller. It
was Harry's own home number, which meant that the
message was no business of mine. I pressed Play anyway.

Amanda Ohlman began speaking from the little plastic
box. "Hi, Dad. Ms. Kiefner had to go out this evening,
so I'm here by myself. Thought I'd give you a call. I had
my personal best in the four hundred today, but the coach
still isn't going to use me in the meet. I got a ninety-
eight on my Spanish test. I was supposed to have pizza

tonight, but I burned it, so I had something else. And I don't mean burned pizza either—ha, ha—I mean something else completely different.

"Guess I'm rambling. I miss you. Take care of yourself. And take care of Uncle Owen. Tell him to take care of you. Then everybody will be covered. Love you. Bye."

The sound of Amanda's voice, more and more like her mother's, should have warmed me, but it didn't. I crossed to the wall of windows and looked down at the reservoir. Harry had been correctly informed, as usual. The jogging trail was brightly lit. The water reflected the regularly spaced halogen lights and others from the hotel and even the moon, though it was almost lost in the crowd.

The memory that had been waiting for its chance ever since Garrity had mentioned my long-ago alibi, the memory I'd held off with my reverie about Mary, ambushed me now. My tired legs were a tangible link to the night in question, the night in March 1969 when Francine Knaff was raped.

I'D WALKED all over Cleveland Circle that night, wandering the rabbit warren of streets between Commonwealth and Beacon. The parking spaces in that neighborhood—a jumbled area of apartments and doubles and single-family homes—were more efficiently used than farmland in Japan, so the sidewalk I followed was shielded from traffic by an unbroken line of cars. Of the people belonging to the cars, there was no sign. That might have been due to the rain, a spring rain as steady as any bathroom shower. Or the residents might just have known better than to walk the streets at night.

Getting mugged worried me about as much as getting wet. The rain was a perfect fit for my mood, which was one of deep self-pity. A knock on the head would have been icing on the cake, absolute proof for the irrational theory I was nursing that life had it in for me.

I somehow ended up on Sutherland Road about the time being wet was starting to lose its romance. I was on the high end of Sutherland, in terms of both topography and house numbers. I descended the steep curving street and came upon a crime scene: police cars and an ambulance blocking the road, just at my building.

I forgot myself in a second and ran to the lights, pressing into the small crowd of onlookers. The police and ambulance men were working in the alley next to Two Sutherland. Their cordon—a single gruff patrolman with an elasticized plastic cover on his hat—prevented me from seeing anything useful.

I changed tactics, entering the building after explaining myself to a second policeman. I was vouched for by Foley the resident assistant, who called after me as I charged up the stairs, "Owen boy, you're soaking!"

Once on three, I entered the empty kitchen and then the service stairs beyond, from which Avery had delivered his unsuccessful defense of Steven Stapella. On its landing was a small window I knew well. Harry had hung me from it when an ill-advised experiment with filterless cigarettes had nearly cost me my dinner. I knew from that exercise that the window overlooked the alley.

I raised the sash carefully and stuck my head out, holding my breath. As I'd hoped, I was directly above the knot of men I'd seen from the street. They circled a figure who had been strapped to a stretcher. One of the men was shielding the figure's face from the rain with a small umbrella.

When the attendants moved to the ends of the stretcher, the man with the umbrella stepped away. I saw a face,

as swollen and red as a newborn's, fringed in wild hair
that was red with blood in spite of the rain. The face was
staring up at me, though its eyes were only slits. It rushed
toward me suddenly as the stretcher was lifted.

I drew my head back inside. Then I stumbled into the
kitchen and threw up in the sink.

TEN

THE NEXT MORNING, Tuesday morning, Harry and I ate a late breakfast in the Dominion's least fussy restaurant. It overlooked the reservoir and was called Le Petit Café, though there was nothing petite about it. Without asking, we were given a table near the inevitable panoramic windows, the better to enjoy the view of Chestnut Hill's future bathwater. We both passed on the café's famous breakfast buffet. Harry ordered fruit and granola and then scowled at me while I ran on at length about how I wanted my eggs cooked. When I began to give similar instructions for my bacon, he figured out that I was only doing it to elicit the scowl, which ruined the game.

After the waitress had brought us some coffee, Harry told me about his family dinner in enough detail to make me happier about my lonely evening. In exchange, I described my one living breathing companion, Melanie Murray.

"Rita Murray told us the truth," I said when I'd finished reconstructing the conversation. "Melanie is obsessing on the rape, not the murder."

"Like Phyllis Garrity," Harry observed. "It's easier to understand in Melanie's case. Her own father, poor kid. And she wasn't exactly on the best of terms with him when he died. That's a whole other pit."

One he knew well, I thought. The memory of it quieted him until his fruit cup arrived. He wolfed down everything but the pineapple chunks and then said, "I think we should talk to Rita Murray again."

"I promised Melanie I wouldn't tell her mother she'd contacted us."

"We don't have to mention that."

"What's the point then?"

"We can ask her about Garrity's claim that she didn't contact Murray in connection with this book she's writing. That sounds thin to me."

I doctored my second cup of coffee. "Garrity didn't contact us about her book either. You would have been easy to trace through the college."

"She also didn't test our DNA, if your theory is correct. She only tested Murray's. So it's possible she only spoke with him. Rita may be able to tell us. Or she may know something about this secret connection between Murray and Garrity you're positing. Talking to her will at least give us something to do. We're spinning our wheels until we hear back about the DNA labs."

My breakfast arrived, cooked to my bogus specifications and garnished with parsley and orange slices. I ate and thought about Harry's real reasons for wanting to revisit Rita Murray. To test a theory, I said, "It might spook Mrs. Murray if both of us show up again. Maybe you should go alone."

"Good thinking. I could pass it off as a social call. Ask her to lunch maybe. She might be more willing to talk that way."

"It's worth a try," I said, thinking I might soon have an interesting voice mail to leave Amanda.

"While I'm gone," Harry said, "there's something you can be mulling over."

"World peace?"

"A way to approach Garrity's husband, Wayne Woodson. If Garrity switched the hair samples to protect the murderer, it has to be someone she'd care about protecting. We can't know why yet, to quote your immortal pronouncement, but maybe we can stir things up. Think of an opening line we can use that doesn't sound like an accusation of murder.''

"Okay," I said.

I sat batting it around and drinking coffee for a while after Harry had gone off to make his arrangements with the Widow Murray. The waitress asked if I wanted anything else every time she refilled my coffee cup. Finally I said, ''A phone. I suppose there's one in the lobby.''

"One moment, sir." She returned carrying a boxy handset with a black rubber antenna.

I thanked her, mentally increasing the tip I'd charge to the suite. Then I called directory assistance and asked for the number of James Corbett. When the operator asked me to be more specific, I dredged up a fragment of address I didn't use too often, a town name, Watertown. The reward for that feat was a computerized woman's voice reading off the number.

An uncomputerized woman answered the number. A very uncomputerized woman, I had reason to believe. One who was seventy or thereabouts. I asked for James Corbett, and she told me that he was out.

''Is this Mrs. Corbett? My name is Owen Keane. I was a student of your husband's at BC. I'm in Boston on business and I was hoping to see him.''

"He's teaching now," Mrs. Corbett said. "He'll be teaching until ten o'clock. Tuesdays and Thursdays nine to ten. The novels of Ross Macdonald."

"Where?"

"At the college. At Carney Hall," she said, slightly exasperated. "I don't know the room number."

"At Boston College? I understood he'd retired."

"He did, but that doesn't stop him from teaching. Not

altogether. Professor emeritus, they call him. He'll never quit. How else could he get young women to come and sit still so he can stare at them for an hour at a time?''

"Beats me," I said.

I treated myself to a cab for the short trip to the campus. It was worth disappointing the driver for a chance to get there before Corbett disappeared. I presented myself, out of breath, to the English department secretary on the third floor of Carney and got the room number of Corbett's class. It was only a few doors away. I might have heard Corbett's deep voice if the blood hadn't been pounding in my ears.

I had five minutes to kill in the crowded hallway, which I passed reading notices on a bulletin board. One in particular caught my eye, a poster advertising teaching assistantships at a college in Kalamazoo, Michigan.

I fell into thinking about what a simple ordinary life in Kalamazoo might be like. From there, it was only a short step to wondering what my life would be like if I'd chosen some graduate school over the seminary all those years ago. Where would I be right now? For once, I knew the answer. I knew that whatever path I'd chosen after Boston College, I would have ended up back on the third floor of Carney. James Murray would still be dead, and nothing I'd done in any parallel life would have absolved me from my part in that. Wherever I might have been when Harry called me with the news, I would have been obligated to come.

A bell rang. Up and down the hallway, classroom doors opened. I was pleased to see that Corbett's door opened last, that his students had enough respect for him to sit still until he reached a period.

I waited until Corbett came marching out, the sight of him yanking me backward as powerfully as anything on the campus or in the city had. He'd been in his fifties when I'd studied with him, and he'd seemed old to me then, as had anyone over thirty. He'd been a big man, powerfully built, who wore his clothes like a schoolboy whose parents couldn't keep up with his growth. He still wore them that way, I was glad to see. His thin hair, brushed straight back from his ruddy face, had whitened, and his glasses had thickened. Otherwise, he seemed unchanged.

I wasn't. Corbett didn't recognize me when I stepped up. Even when I'd given him my name, he kept on staring at me like he wanted to ask for my driver's license.

"It's been years since your last letter," he eventually said. "I wasn't sure I'd hear from you again. And now you're here. Let me see, you were working for a newspaper, weren't you?"

"I was," I said, telling him all he needed to know about that résumé entry.

He put a big hand on my shoulder, steering me down the crowded hallway. "That's why I insisted you start dating your letters," he said as we hiked. "I file my correspondence and I like to keep everything in order. With most of my old students' letters, I can work the chronology out from internal evidence. So-and-so's an assistant something or other. Assistant vice president, say. Then vice president, then senior vice president. But your career has a certain nonlinear quality."

He showed me into an office whose cinder block walls were decorated with notices of campus events, some of them ancient: concerts and readings and plays. One of the posters gave me a small start. It promoted a campus production of *Hamlet,* James Murray's debut play. When I noticed that this effort had been staged in 1994, I relaxed.

Corbett hadn't relaxed, not completely. He was still watching me warily through his welder's glasses as he squeezed in behind the office's little metal desk. He hadn't removed his plaid woolen sports coat, though the office was warm. He fingered at the knot of his tie with fat blunt fingers. The tie was already loose and his collar was open. Or sprung.

I hadn't returned to the suite to collect my new topcoat on my way out of the Dominion. I hadn't wanted to bump into Harry. The suit I was wearing hadn't traveled well. In fact, it might actually have gotten carsick. Corbett was probably afraid I'd hit him up for a loan.

"Cozy, isn't it?" he said, gesturing around the office. "I share it with a graduate student. Had to give up my real office when I turned seventy. I'm currently hanging on here by my fingernails."

"Teaching Ross Macdonald, I hear."

"Right, right. You know his stuff, of course. You would. I've often wondered what the old Jesuit who hired me forty-five years ago—Father Berry—would say if he knew I'd ended my days lecturing on detective novels."

"It would have depended on whether you could have gotten him to read one."

"Spoken like a true advocate, Owen." He held up the book he'd been carrying with his class notes. *The Blue Hammer*. "This one might have sold him all by itself. Macdonald's classic situation: the dead past reaching forward to shake the present by its throat. God, could he play that tune.

"That reminds me of something that really yanked my chain, something another writer said about Macdonald. Another mystery writer, by God. It was on the order of that famous slam against Antonio Vivaldi, the one that said Vivaldi didn't really write five hundred concertos;

he wrote one concerto five hundred times. This was the same charge, but not as cleverly put. This guy—I forget his name—said that Macdonald had good carbon paper. Do you get it? Good carbon paper.

"Can you imagine another writer saying that? I could accept it from an academic or even a critic. But I'd expect a writer to understand."

"What?" I asked.

"That a writer will return to the same story over and over again because it's the one story he really wants to tell, the one that's most important to him." Corbett banged his big chest. "The one that's in here. That make sense to you?"

"Yes," I said, but without enough enthusiasm. Corbett was now both wary and disappointed.

"I thought at one time that you might have the writing bug, Owen. You've got the eye for it. And you loved books, as I recall. Loved them dangerously, the way a writer will. Did you ever consider a writing career?"

"It's the only one I haven't considered," I said.

That admission led me naturally into a recounting of the careers I'd undertaken since I'd sent my last letter to Corbett. The recounting led me in turn to a statement of my current reason for being in Boston. The statement I gave wasn't entirely frank. I told the old man that I'd come to do research and asked him if he knew Wayne Woodson.

"The dean of the deconstructionists? Of course I know him. I mentored him, once upon a time. That was way back in your day. He wasn't tenured then, but he was around. Do you remember him?"

"Vaguely," I said.

"Never took one of his classes, I bet. No. That's easy enough to understand. He was always a firebrand," Corbett said, echoing Mustafa's assessment of Phyllis Garrity. "A life and death approach to everything."

"Life and death?" I asked.

"Intense, I mean. And a tough grader. 'Woe-is-me Woodson,' the kids call him. Or 'Doctor D Minus.' No offense, Owen, but you were always a lazy kind of student. Too busy with your own concerns to take your classes very seriously. You were happier with easygoing old hands like me. And you enjoyed literature. I'm not sure Woodson does, for all his success. That's hurt us, hurt the department."

"How?"

"Don't get me gossiping. I can't stop once I start, and my roommate will be here to claim the office any time now. Suffice it to say that Woodson was one of a group of young world-beaters who came to us back in the sixties. They weren't content to labor as assistants for twenty years until all their elders had died off. So they came up with crazy new theories that stood all the great books and poems on their heads. Turned them all inside out, their meanings inside out. Yanked their truths right out of them so they could be loaded down with ideological freight the original authors never dreamed of.

"I didn't see it at the time, but those young radicals were like the wasps you see on the nature shows, the ones who plant their larvae in the living body of some fat dumb worm. I'm pretty sure it's wasps I mean. The larvae eat the worm alive from the inside out, leaving a worm skin bursting with wasps. That's what happened to our department. One day the skin burst and the wasps were running the place. They were..."

His insect imagery failed him for the moment. "Being asked to sit on Pulitzer Prize committees?" I suggested.

"Right," Corbett said, his wariness returning. "What's your interest in old Woe-is-me?"

"I'm interested in deconstruction," I said.

"You? Hmmm." Now the wariness was tempered by something else: a desire to pass the Owen Keane buck. "Well, you'll never understand it listening to me. I've developed a mental block on the subject. You should go right to the source. Would you like an introduction to Dr. Woodson?"

"Please," I said.

Corbett opened a desk drawer and banged about. "Can never find that department schedule. Can never read it when I find it; the new computer prints so itty-bitty." He picked up his phone and pressed a single button. "Grace? Is his highness in today? Is he free? Sure, I can hold."

He put his hand over the receiver. "The joke's on the wasps, that's what I think. Yes, they overturned the scholarship. Yes, they gutted the great books. Yes, they won all the chairs and the honors. But they lost most of the students. They'll never know what it's like to teach someone like you, someone who really loves the material. They have to make do with young radicals, as hungry as they once were, who can't wait to replace their theories with even crazier ones.

"Yes, Grace, I'm still here. I'll be here till they carry me out. Is Woodson receiving? Good. We're on our way."

ELEVEN

As I FOLLOWED Corbett into a private suite of offices that were defended by Grace the department secretary against the walk-in trade, I asked myself whether Harry would accept the excuse that I'd exceeded my brief because I'd been swept along by events. Then I asked myself whether that was even true, whether I would have gone back to the Dominion if I'd missed Corbett or simply knocked unannounced on Woodson's door.

Before I could decide, Corbett was tapping with a fleshy hand on the frame of that same door, looking like an overgrown kid again, a kid who had been called to the principal's office. For all his vague talk about mentoring Woodson, the professor emeritus was intimidated by the younger man. That revelation did nothing to steel my nerves.

"Wayne, got a minute? There's someone I'd like you to meet. A former student of mine, Owen Keane. He's interested in deconstruction."

That was all the leg up Corbett gave me before hurrying away. I received even less orientation from Woodson. I expected him to mention my encounter with his wife the previous day. Or to give me a chance to mention it. Instead, the man lounging behind the desk launched into a meditation.

"Odd your showing up now. I was just pondering on deconstruction in the broadest sense. I'm afraid it's becoming a catch-all term for a host of new critical theories. For example, I was just reading an essay about absence.

That's one of the hot new ideas, that you can learn a lot about a work by considering what the author left out. This particular piece concerns absences in *Robinson Crusoe*. It's about the items Crusoe doesn't save from the wreck and doesn't find on the island. And—more broadly—it's about the social issues of the time that Daniel Defoe doesn't mention in the book.''

Woodson was less august in person than his photo in the *Alumni Report*. The diminished presence might have been due to his speaking voice, which was very nearly prepubescent. Or it might have been a trick of the office's indifferent fluorescent lighting. The pebbled ceiling fixtures were the only things the office had in common with Corbett's, perhaps the only things the college had provided, aside from the walls and the floor. The brown and blue oriental rug on which I stood, the cherry desk behind which Woodson reclined in a leather wing chair, the framed artwork on the walls, all struck me as little touches of home.

''What you end up with when you consider a story's absences may be a new view of the original book. A photographic negative for the picture Defoe took of his time. Or it may be a completely new creative work. What's your opinion?''

I voted for option B, thinking that the author of the essay should have written his own novel and left Defoe's alone. That would have gone badly with my pose as a seeker of enlightenment, so I said, ''It's an intriguing idea.''

''It surprises me to hear you say so. Have a seat, by the way. I would have expected someone your age—especially a student of that famous mossback James Corbett—to be a disciple of imagery and theme and metaphor. A worshiper of the text. Someone naturally hostile to the deconstructing of texts.''

I was too busy adjusting myself to the sensory difference between Corbett's hard plastic chair and Woodson's soft leather one to see what was coming.

"But then, you're fairly eclectic, aren't you, Mr. Keane? Just yesterday you were interested in the psychology of rape. Today it's deconstruction. What's the link?''

"A natural curiosity," I said.

"Yes, my wife mentioned that about you." He gestured to the framed work of art that hung closest to his desk. It was a double portrait, done in pastels, of a much younger Garrity and a beaming little girl of four or five.

"Beautiful, wasn't she?''

"Yes," I said, because it was so obviously true. Garrity had been a striking young woman, at least to the artist's eye, her skin unmarked, her body straight and full, her dark hair shining to an extraordinary degree, given the dull medium of the portrait.

"The little girl is our daughter, Bergen," Woodson said. "She's a book editor now. Computer manuals," he added, shaking his head. "All my discussions with her about literature over the years, and she ends up thinking of the English language as just another code for conveying useful information. Corbett teases me about that when he's feeling bold. He considers it a victory for his side.''

He paused, inviting me to rub it in, too. I was thinking of the problems James Murray had had with Melanie. In comparison, Woodson's disappointments were as comfortable as his furniture.

"As to defining deconstruction in twenty-five words or less, Mr. Keane, I can more easily tell you what it isn't. It isn't what James Corbett thinks it is. It isn't academic

game playing. It isn't wanton destruction by a gang of
unruly children intent on pulling their father's watch
apart with no plan for putting it back together again. Corbett sees deconstruction as one more sign that the world
is going to hell around him, which is the disease of all
old people. It's of a piece with his feet hurting and his
bowel movements becoming irregular and ice cream not
tasting like it did when he was a boy.''

I stirred finally in my easy chair. ''Does the formal
definition actually mention Corbett's bowel movements?''

Woodson laughed easily. ''I don't know that there is
a formal definition. The simplest one might be that deconstruction is a denial of—or at least a challenge to—
the assumption that underlay all previous criticism. The
assumption being that literary texts possess meaning and
that literary criticism is the process of discovering that
meaning.

''You've heard, of course, of Jacques Derrida. He is
in many ways the father of deconstruction. One of his
basic ideas, *differance,* may be of particular interest to
you. The term combines the senses of both *difference* and
deferral, as follows. A thing is defined by how it differs
from other things. No thing is known in itself. We move
from one unknown thing to the next, our definitions
breaking down at every move. Truth always steps back
as we approach, according to Derrida. The final answer
is always deferred, never reached.''

''Sounds like a guy I could split a six-pack with.'' Of
particular interest to me, Woodson had said. Either he
was an extremely quick study or Garrity had briefed him
well, having been briefed herself by the old case file. My
1969 police interrogations must have been more thorough
than I remembered.

To give me time to find my feet, I added, "Reminds me of Zeno's paradox."

"Which one?" Woodson asked. "There were several."

"The one that says that motion is impossible because before you can get from point A to point B you first have to travel half the distance, but before you can do that, you first have to travel halfway to the halfway point, and so on. Because the distance can be subdivided an infinite number of times, you can never make any progress."

Woodson restated the paradox more succinctly. "You can't transverse an infinite number of points in a finite amount of time."

"Another old Greek had a simple answer for Zeno, as I recall."

The professor knew it. "'It is disproved by walking.' Are you saying there is an equivalent reply to Derrida's proposition that we can never know the truth because it withdraws as we advance? What would it be? 'It is disproved by reading'?"

"That would work fine for the truths of books or poems," I said. "For truth in general, you might just say, 'It is disproved by living.'"

Woodson and I stared at one another for a time, each wondering if the other had seen through his bluff. That's what I was wondering, anyway. I heard a muffled explosion of laughter from a classroom on the floor below and wished I was down there, studying Cervantes or Fielding. The wish wasn't granted.

"I have to correct you on one point," I said. "I wouldn't want to leave you with the wrong idea. You said earlier that I approached your wife to learn about the psychology of rape. That's not really true. My friend

Harry Ohlman and I looked her up to ask about an evidence file she'd had in her possession.''

"The Cleveland Circle file,'' Woodson said, suddenly impatient now that we'd arrived at the real point of my visit.

"You knew about the case? Prior to your wife's mentioning our call?''

"Of course. I've lived with her latest work in progress for years, just as she's lived with mine.''

"Did you examine the evidence file? Or the case file?'' Maybe Garrity hadn't briefed him on me after all. Maybe he'd done his own research.

"No and no,'' Woodson said. "Absolutely not.''

"Your wife never left them lying around the breakfast nook?''

"She kept all that material locked up in her office, as I believe she told you herself.''

"Now that you mention it. Did you know James Courtney Murray?''

"I recently heard the name from my wife. After his murder. I never met the man. Why would I have?''

"He was a student here.''

"Not a student of mine. Not that I recall. Now, if you'll excuse me, Mr. Keane, I have to review some lecture notes. If you've any real curiosity about deconstruction, I could provide you with a short reading list. You could come back in, say, a month to discuss it again.''

I stood up. "I'll only be here for a day or two,'' I said. "And I've other things to occupy me.''

"You're like the man in Zeno's dilemma, then,'' Woodson observed, his noblesse oblige back in full bloom. "An infinite number of points to cross in a finite amount of time. You'll have to walk quickly.''

TWELVE

I took Woodson's advice and set a brisk pace for my walk back to the Dominion. I would have hustled in any case. The day had gone overcast, and there was enough moisture in the wind for the word snow to form in the back of my mind. I thought of phoning for a courtesy car, as Harry had done, but my interview with the specialist in deconstruction had left me feeling a little down at the heel. I could picture the driver of the big Lincoln passing me by without slowing.

For once the humid warmth of the hotel's rain forest lobby was welcome. Less so was the sight of a figure in a pea jacket hunched in one of the armchairs near the goldfish pond. Melanie Murray. She'd let me off too easily the night before. Now she was back to give me another opportunity to tell her more than I should.

When I got closer, I decided she might actually have come for first aid. She was pale, but I already thought of that as her defining characteristic. What disturbed me more was the impression that her head was being held upright only by the stiff collar of her coat. I was also bothered by the swollen look of her heavily made-up eyes. What I could see beyond the thick lashes was more pink than white.

"You okay?" I asked.

"I told you I'm not big on daylight."

"I thought only vampires took it this hard."

"Don't tell me you've never had a hangover."

That explained the empty ashtray. "I can't tell you

that," I said. "Several of my early ones are in local museums."

Melanie blinked up at me, smiling or grimacing; I couldn't tell which. "Then you should know a cure."

I did. It was the same cure she was facing for the pain of her father's death. She had to outlive it. That wasn't what she wanted to hear, so I said, "I prescribe lunch. Come on."

Le Petit Café was doing a booming lunch trade, much of it made up of business people in well dressed, noisy groups. Luckily, the table near the windows where Harry and I had breakfasted was being bused as Melanie and I walked up. The view was wasted on my guest, who donned a pair of sunglasses as we sat down, though the day was darkening steadily. The hostess asked if she could take Melanie's coat and was more or less ignored. She tried for a drink order next and got my companion's full attention. I guessed that Melanie was figuring the odds of getting carded if she ordered something alcoholic. I asked for decaf coffee while she was doing the math, which must have discouraged her. She waved the hostess away.

"She'll have an orange juice," I said. "The biggest you have."

"Is that part of the cure?" Melanie asked. "Or are you just trying to change the color of my puke?"

I opened her menu and held it out to her. "After that question, I won't ask you what looks good. Just pick something without sharp corners."

She ordered an omelet and I asked for a club sandwich from the same waitress who had served Harry and me at breakfast. She didn't ask what I was doing back there so soon. She didn't appear to remember me. James Corbett still remembered the college Keane after two decades, but

I hadn't lasted in this woman's mind for two hours. I suppressed a sigh.

The forgetful waitress had brought our drinks, and Melanie was sipping hers before we were alone again. She sipped so long that my attention wandered. She set the glass down hard to draw me back from a reverie inspired by the reservoir.

"Did you drink with my father when you two were freshmen?"

Wary of a trap, I said, "Sometimes. Early in that first semester. It was all for one and one for all at first. We hadn't realized yet that all of us landing on the same floor of the same dorm really didn't mean anything. That we weren't really a unit. If one of us drank, we all drank."

"Drank what?" Melanie asked. Half of her milkshake-size orange juice was already gone.

"Beer. Budweiser, usually. That was your father's favorite back then."

"You said last night you admired his sophistication. Budweiser doesn't sound very sophisticated."

"Sophistication is a quality, not a brand name. Your father knew how to drink, which was more impressive to me than what he drank."

"Guess I didn't inherit that gene," Melanie said.

The waitress came by with a coffee refill and several follow-up questions regarding Melanie's omelet. Once more I was distracted by the view.

"You're staring out the window again," Melanie said, unamused. "Am I that messed up, or do you have a thing for water?"

"Only this water. This reservoir was an important landmark for Harry Ohlman and me. I'm finding it a little hard to believe I'm back here again."

"Tell me the story."

I couldn't. For the reservoir story to make sense, I would have to discuss her father's innocence, and I was determined not to do that. Not yet.

"We were talking about drinking. I did okay with that while I stayed with the Budweiser herd. But Harry and I strayed late in our first semester. To scotch. I think it was the night before we were all going home for Thanksgiving. I can't remember how we came by the bottle, a fifth. We didn't drink the whole thing, but it might have been better for me if we had. Then I wouldn't have been ambulatory enough to visit a party a girl I knew was throwing on the floor below us. She was serving a punch made with apple wine. Apple wine is what nondrinkers drank before someone invented wine coolers."

"Stop," Melanie said, holding up small hands. "I know what's coming. What do you do for headaches, Dr. Keane? Play the drums?"

"It's called aversion therapy. Shall I go on? The part where I tried to ride the trolley to the bus station the next morning is especially moving."

"Just cut to the moral. You and Mr. Ohlman never drank scotch again."

Harry and I *had* sworn off scotch, but we'd neglected to throw out the rest of the bottle. A month or so later we'd finished it, the first of many emptied scotch bottles for me. I was prepared to lie about it for a good cause, to tell Melanie I'd stayed sober and lived happily ever after. I was in a better position to tell that lie than James Murray had been. According to his wife, he'd lived his life much the way I remembered him spending his college days. Never quite drunk, never quite sober.

"Did your father's drinking bother you?" I asked.

Melanie might have shrugged, though the shoulders of

her pea jacket didn't move. "Maybe he had good reason to drink. It seems he did," she added, trying to steer me.

"What's your excuse?"

"Same one. Cleveland Circle. Call it my inheritance."

"You were drinking before you'd ever heard that story."

That surprised her, but only briefly. "I forgot you'd talked to my mother. Did you tell her why you'd really come to Boston?"

"We told her about the audit."

"Don't give me that shit again. I'm talking about the real reason. Why can't you stick to the truth?"

Because it always moved away as I approached it. I'd known about that phenomenon before I'd ever heard of Jacques Derrida. But it had never kept me from taking the next step.

"We don't know the truth about your father's death," I said. "If we find out anything, we'll tell you. We'll tell your mother. In the meantime, you may be able to help us."

"How?"

"Have you ever heard the name Phyllis Garrity?"

"No," Melanie said quickly. She thought about it and came up with the same answer. "Who is she?"

"Someone who might have tried to get in touch with your father. How about Wayne Woodson?"

"Sounds made up. No, I never heard of him either. What did they want with my father?"

"Nothing maybe. We're still working it out."

"I get it. You can ask questions and I can't. It's like drinking."

Her accusation made me smile. "You can't blame me for warning you off my bad habits. Did your father seem worried about anything in the month or so before he died?''

"You mean besides me and my drinking? No, not that I noticed.''

Lunch arrived. Melanie asked for cayenne pepper sauce, doused her omelet with it, and then shoved it away.

She allowed me to eat half my sandwich. Then she said, "You tricked me just now."

"Orange juice always worked for me."

"I'm not talking about the orange juice. When I asked you for the truth, you said you didn't know the truth about my father's death. But that's not the whole story. Do you know the truth about what happened at Cleveland Circle?"

I pushed my plate over to join hers, deciding without knowing why that I had to give her something to hold on to. "Yes."

"Did James Murray commit that crime?"

"No."

Whatever had been holding her up against the tug of the hangover drained out of her. She slumped in her chair. "How do you know?"

"That's all I'm going to tell you for the moment, Melanie. It has to hold you for a while. I may have told you too much already. I don't want you interfering and messing things up. You have to give us a couple more days to do our job."

"What is your job? Mr. Ohlman is a lawyer, but what are you?"

"I do research for a historical society," I said, giving her the most recent answer.

"You're not a policeman?"

"No."

"Or a detective?"

"No," I said, smiling again. "What made you ask that?"

"You said just now that asking questions was one of your bad habits. I thought it might be your job."

"You're not as out of it as you look. Asking questions is more like my avocation. My hobby."

"I know what avocation means. Don't talk down to me, okay?"

"Sorry."

"Did you have the same avocation when you were in college?"

"Yes."

"Did you ask questions about the Cleveland Circle rape?"

"Yes." I knew I'd have to start talking or she'd get everything out of me, one monosyllable at a time. "It was a difficult case. The best clues were some stray hairs that had gotten wrapped around a ring on the victim's hand."

"Francine Knaff's hand," Melanie said. "She had a name."

"I know her name," I said. "The only thing the police had beside those hairs was a key found near the body. It was a key to the front door of our dorm. Your father's and mine and Mr. Ohlman's. It might have been dropped by the rapist. Or it might already have been lying there when she was attacked."

"The police couldn't tell whose key it was?"

"No. The Cleveland Circle housing had been arranged at the last minute by the college. Everything had been rushed together. Improvised. The keys we were given weren't numbered or even accounted for very well. Nobody knew exactly how many had been made or handed out. There were extras kept in the resident assistant's room, in an unlocked desk drawer. That was considered an important point, because when the police got around to checking, every dorm resident had a key.''

''What about fingerprints on the key? Was it too small?''

''And too wet,'' I said. ''That was the big problem with the crime scene. It rained that night like it rains in the tropics. A lot of the evidence just washed away.''

''Including Francine Knaff's blood?''

''No,'' I said, seeing again the wild red hair. ''There was too much of that.''

Melanie stood up. ''I need air.'' I started to get up, too. ''No. I mean I need to be alone. I'll be back for the rest of the story.''

When I least expected it, I thought. ''Go easy on yourself till then,'' I said.

THIRTEEN

THERE WAS A LINE of people waiting for tables at the café's entrance. I gave mine up with a parting glance at the slate gray water beyond the glass. I intended to go up to the suite to wait for Harry, but I didn't make it. On my way to the elevators, I spotted a bar. The Last Stand.

Potted palms flanked the entrance, an archway crowned with the emblem of some famous or forgotten or fictitious regiment. I went in, noting first the brass and the blue velour of the furniture, then the spears and arrows and rifles mounted on the dark-papered walls. The Last Stand wasn't as busy as the café had been, which I took as a sign of the health-conscious times. I found a relatively private seat at the bar, across from an old print depicting a battle identified as "Isandhlwana." The combatants were African natives and soldiers in red coats and white pith helmets. The Africans looked to be kicking butt.

When the bartender came by, I was tempted to order a scotch, my storytelling for Melanie having revived the old thirst. I ordered a beer instead, a Budweiser, in honor of Melanie's father. As I sipped it, I thought back on a conversation I'd had with Murray a few days after the rape of Francine Knaff.

MARY AND I had been sitting together on the steps of the service stairs of Two Sutherland, near the window from which I'd seen Knaff's body. I was keeping tabs on a project going on in the alley below. Two workmen, under the watchful eye of a policeman, had pulled up the cover of a drain set in the alley's concrete floor. They were taking turns fishing in the drain with a length of wire.

Murray came out of the kitchen just as I was drawing my head in after my latest check on their progress.

"They find anything?" he asked, loudly enough, I thought, to be heard below street level.

I started to shut the window. "No," I said.

Murray stopped me and stuck his head out. "'Foul deeds will rise, though all the earth o'erwhelm them to men's eyes,'" he called out. "Women's eyes, too," he said to Mary after he'd slammed the window shut. "Hi, Fitz."

"Hi, J.C.," she said.

"Where's that roommate of yours been hiding, Keane? I want to get his take on the inquisition. Did they ask him the same questions they asked us?"

"Yes," I said, though I had no idea what questions Harry had been asked for the simple reason that he hadn't said two words to me since the night of the attack.

The preliminary interviews had been conducted in our own building, in the first-floor room set aside as the dorm lounge. The examiners had been a pair of detectives, both of them dressed as though the fifties had never gone away. I'd walked into my interrogation naively expecting to be recognized as a junior colleague. I'd come out shaken and scared.

"He has his key, right? Ohlman?"

"Yes," I said.

Every male in the dorm had been asked to produce his front door key for examination. When that hadn't resulted in an identification, the police had checked the keys of all the women on the theory that a trusting coed might

have lent hers to her boyfriend. That hadn't worked out
for them either.

I sat down next to Mary. Murray leaned against the
banister above us. "There are those extra keys in Foley's
room," he said, thinking aloud. "But he's kept his door
locked since his television walked away in January."

Mary reached into her jeans pocket, stretching her legs
out on the stairs and leaning backward slightly to create
the required slack. She extracted a piece of paper and
handed it to Murray.

"'From the desk of Thomas Foley,'" Murray read.

"Owen got that this morning while Foley was at
breakfast. He opened Foley's door with a cafeteria pass.
I stood guard."

"The extra keys weren't in there this morning," Murray said. "The campus cops took them away."

"They were in there the morning after the attack," I
said. "I wanted to see if someone could have gotten in
there and taken a key."

Murray was unimpressed. "So we should be frisking
you for the stolen TV. Let's get back to Ohlman. What's
his alibi?"

Every brown-haired man had been asked to provide
one. They were a hotter topic of conversation than our
draft numbers.

Before I was forced to admit that I didn't know Harry's
alibi, Mary said, "He was down in the combat zone."

"The combat zone?" Murray repeated. It was an area
of bars and strip joints not far from the Boston Common.
"Who with?"

"Alone," Mary said. "Looking for a drink."

"Looking for trouble," Murray said. "Something not
right about that."

I agreed. It wasn't right that Mary should know about

it when I hadn't. To shift the subject, I asked Murray about his own alibi, which I'd already heard secondhand.

"Rehearsal. *Measure for Measure.* I'm thinking of dropping out though. The bastards still won't give me a speaking part. And after *Hamlet* everything else seems a little thin. 'Stale, flat, and unprofitable,' you know, which always sounds like a description of old beer.

"Speaking of thin, Keane, you should work on your alibi. It was a lousy night for a stroll. I suggest adding a secret rendezvous with a chick."

Beside me, Mary stirred, drawing Murray's eye. "You going to our two o'clock, Fitz, or cutting? We've just got time to make the shuttle."

"Let me get my notebook," Mary said.

Murray and I walked her down to her room. We waited for her in the hallway that was identical to ours but smelled so much better. Through one of the closed doors I could hear Janis Joplin imploring someone to take another piece of her heart. The record was competing with Murray, who was still on the subject of alibis.

"Old Tregnab's sweating because he was in the library. On a Friday night. Him and two other people probably, both of them nearsighted. He's sure no one will remember him. Avery's got the best story. He drove over to see his folks in Needham. He should be thrilled, but he's not. Guess there was some trouble out there. 'They come not single spies, but in battalions.' Troubles."

"Sorrows," I said, "Not troubles."

"How do you know that?"

"You've used that damn quote once a week since October."

I intended to see them as far as the bus stop, but when we reached the first floor, we ran into Alan Avery, who was coming out of Foley's room. He asked if he could talk to me.

We all left Two Sutherland together, but Avery and I walked east on Beacon, along a broad sidewalk that fronted little shops. As we walked, he flipped open a hardpack of Parliaments and offered me one. I considered it a compliment as well as a cigarette and took it. He passed me his stainless steel Zippo, which I managed to work one-handed on my first try.

We smoked and walked for a time, Avery moving in a rolling gait that forced me to stay well to one side of him. The extra distance made it possible for me to watch him. The distance and the difference in our heights. Shorter than I was, Avery was also heavier, barrel-chested and broad shouldered. His gaze, though cast down, remained intense. One of my beloved private eye paperbacks would have described his heavy brow as knitted. He brushed his hair back from his face every few steps, as characteristic a gesture as Harry's incessant mustache-smoothing, but did it absently.

"Foley's a mess," he finally said. "They're really coming down hard on him over the keys. And over his whereabouts on Friday night."

"Foley?" I asked, as though his lofty status as our resident assistant placed him above suspicion.

"He was reading in his room. The cops think he should have heard something. They don't realize how noisy that building always is. I think they're zeroing in on him because he's a foreigner."

"He's an Irishman in Boston," I said. "That doesn't exactly make him an illegal alien."

Avery took a deep drag on his cigarette and stuck it in the corner of his mouth for safekeeping. "He's acting like one. He may try to give them someone else to get himself off the hot seat. *You*, Keane. That's what I wanted to tell you."

My cigarette, carried in the corner of my mouth, was making my eyes water. I took it out.

"He saw you come in soaking wet on Friday night."

"Everyone was wet on Friday night," I said.

"He said you ran past him without saying anything."

"I wanted to see what was happening. From the stairway window."

"I thought that might be it. The thing is, Keane, Foley doesn't understand you. You're a mystery to him. Now he's facing another mystery and he's getting the two confused. People with issues they don't understand confuse the big ones and the little ones. Ever notice that?"

"No," I said.

"I thought you might not have," he said, then immediately retreated to generalities. "You see it with Vietnam these days. The war's a mystery to most people: why we're over there, why some people are dying, why others get to party on a college campus like nothing's happening. They jumble those questions together with little mysteries—why don't my kids speak to me anymore, how do I get laid, why did my parents waste their lives—and see it all as a unit, a fabric. If they can find one answer, it will answer everything, they think. They don't make answers like that."

We passed a Chinese restaurant and the smell of frying meat came out to us. It reminded me that I hadn't eaten anything all day, with my experiments in lock picking and my supervision of the police. Worse, I'd kept Mary from eating anything.

"The problem is your alibi," Avery said. "You were walking around for a reason that night, but you won't say what it was. That makes everyone suspicious."

"You've got a good alibi," I said.

I was only trying to get myself off the hot seat, as Avery had put it. I came close to ending the entire conversation. My companion flicked his cigarette down the sidewalk. When we reached the spot where it had come to rest, he ground it into the concrete. "I'd trade you mine for yours right now, Keane. As worthless as your story is, I'd rather have it."

"What happened?" I asked, not really expecting him to tell me.

"My parents asked me to come home for the weekend. I knew that meant trouble. They never ask me for social purposes. Not anymore. We had a falling out when I transferred here. Over what isn't important. Since then, when they've talked to me at all it's been about what a disappointment I am to them. That's what I thought I was going to get on Friday night, the standard lecture. It wasn't. My parents told me they're planning to divorce."

"Sorry," I said.

"What's the old saying? 'Turnabout is fair play.' If that's true, I don't deserve anybody's sorrys. My parents must feel that way about it, because they didn't offer me theirs. I haven't told anyone else the particulars, Keane. I'm telling you because I know I can trust you."

"Thanks."

Avery stopped, smiled at a little girl who was sitting in a stroller while her mother visited a shop, and said, "Guess we should turn back."

We walked without speaking for a time. Then Avery suddenly bent down—to tie his shoe, I thought. Instead, he picked something off the sidewalk. It was the cigarette stub he'd left on our eastbound leg. He dropped it in a trash can near the curb. I still carried the remains of my Parliament. I'd been meditating on the brown stain that had formed on the base of the filter. I tossed it in after his.

"You know the craziest thing Foley told the police about you, Keane? It was that late last year, back before his television got stolen, you and Ohlman used to come down to his room most nights to watch the old *Perry Mason* shows they run after the late news."

"We did," I said.

"According to Foley, you always knew who the murderer was. Ohlman once in a while, but you always. To Foley, that was unnatural. Or supernatural. Or a sign of a criminal mind."

"Maybe it is," I said.

"You might consider putting that talent to use now. It might be important for you to. I know you're playing at solving this the way you seem to play at most things. I saw you and the Fitzgerald girl fooling around Foley's room this morning. You might want to get serious for a change. If you've got a talent for picking out a murderer, you should use it."

"We're looking for a rapist," I said.

"Not anymore. Francine Knaff died early this morning. Foley just got the word."

FOURTEEN

PICK OUT the murderer. It was easy enough when I had Raymond Burr to identify the suspects for me and question them under oath. Now I had to make do with the Boston police, who weren't as forthcoming. At least not about the results of their interrogations.

I only knew the details of my own callback, which took place—on the day after Knaff died—at police headquarters on Berkeley Street. Headquarters was a formal old stone building whose looks were spoiled for me by the green iron gratings on its lower story windows. My interview was conducted by two plainclothesmen I hadn't met before, Kossel and Craney, two more wetheads in bad suits, though Craney, the shorter of the pair, took his suit coat off immediately to show off his bowler's forearms.

Kossel did most of the talking while the bowler sat and glowered at me. Without actually saying so, Kossel managed to convey the idea that Craney wanted to beat the truth out of me and only his partner's benevolence was holding him back. I knew the good cop/bad cop dodge by heart, but I still believed Kossel completely. Nevertheless, I stuck to the only story I had, the one I'd told their predecessors in the lounge at Two Sutherland.

The intimidation continued when the interrogators passed me to the technician assigned to take my voluntary hair sample. Craney escorted me to a dirty room with exposed steam pipes in one corner, the pipes wrapped in insulation that had been painted the same mud brown as the walls. The detective sat himself on the room's only furniture, a metal table, and addressed the man with the shears, a uniformed cop who wore the smell of dried sweat like a favorite cologne.

"A healthy sample," Craney said. "He can afford it. But be discreet."

"Okay," the cop said, smiling broadly. He took the heavy lock I wore across my forehead in his hand and cut it off with a single pass of his hedge clippers. "Discreet enough?"

"Hardly noticeable," Craney said. "Don't forget the type two."

"Right. Look down at your shoes, kid."

I did, expecting him to chop away at the hair on the top of my head. I felt him separate a few strands and draw them taut. He raised the shears, but didn't cut with them. It felt like he was winding the hairs around the closed blades. Before I could ask him what he was doing, he yanked the shears upward, pushing my head down with his free hand. I yelped with pain as the hairs pulled free.

"Take you back to that night in the alley?" Craney asked. "Or were you too busy beating that nurse to notice?"

"His eyes are tearing," the barber noted happily. "Didn't hurt you, did I?"

"Yeah," I said. "You exposed both armpits at once."

I expected him to hit me then. He looked to Craney for permission, but the detective was busy clearing his throat. When he finished, he said, "Get out."

The same treatment was given to every man from Two Sutherland who was called back for a second interrogation. The vandalism worked to my advantage, as it identified every brown-haired man in the dorm whose alibi was weak. There were eight of us semifinalists. Foley and a freshman named Newcomb on the first floor, two more freshmen, Cully and Riggio, on Avery's fifth floor, and four on the lucky third: Tregnab, Murray, Harry, and I.

Because Avery had tipped me to Foley's plight, the big surprise on that list was Murray. I thought his rehearsal alibi was second only to Avery's, given the number of people in the cast of *Measure for Measure*. But when I returned to the dorm from my second interview, I found that Murray had been given an even worse shearing. Being Murray, he was joking about it—letting in the sunlight would help dry up his acne—but he was drinking, too, at three in the afternoon.

Harry, who had been accompanied to his questioning by his lawyer father, up from New York, didn't get back until after dinner. When he walked in, I saw that part of his afternoon had been spent with a real barber who had severely trimmed his hair to hide the hatchet work of the police. Harry paused near the foot of the bed where I lay reading to let me comment, looking at me with less love than Craney had shown. When I didn't say anything, he took his clarinet out onto the glassed-in porch, shutting the door behind him. I waited for him to begin playing, but he never did.

I DECIDED to start with Tregnab. I told myself it was because the next day was Friday and I needed a Friday to check his story. But it might have been because, of all the suspects, he was the one I would have least minded turning in.

My plan was to go to Bapst Library after dinner and stay there until closing time—as Tregnab claimed to have done. I was fairly certain that the same staff would be on duty. I was hoping I might even find some students who

had been there the night of the attack, Friday night studying being, it seemed to me, pretty much a lifestyle choice.

I didn't bother preparing a clever story to explain my
interest in Tregnab's study habits. I couldn't think of one
that would have gotten people talking as effectively as
the truth, the murder, a subject I heard discussed everywhere I went on campus.

According to Tregnab's own account, which he'd nervously told over and over during the week, he'd been
studying in the basement stacks, where the lighting was
bad but the quiet absolute. So, when I arrived at Bapst,
a building that was mistaken for a church by every new
visitor to the campus, I descended the curving stone stairs
to the basement. I started with the guardian of the stacks,
a graduate student who worked the front desk. His name
was Janklow, and I knew him well enough to nod to him
during my own visits. He was tall and thin, dressed half
a decade out of date in chinos, madras shirts, and desert
boots, wore oversize glasses, and patronized a barber as
reactionary as the one who had repaired Harry.

I told Janklow I was looking into the Knaff murder
and why. It made his Friday night.

"You're a suspect in a murder and you have to solve
it to clear yourself?" he asked. "That sounds like the
plot of a detective novel we have down here. Which one
is it?" He snapped his fingers and pretended to think.
"It's, it's, it's—Wait a minute, it's all of them."

"Good one," I said. "Keep in mind how they all end
and stay on the side of right."

"By telling you what?"

I described Tregnab and asked the librarian if he'd
seen him on the previous Friday night.

"You need a photograph," he said. "You underclass-
men all look alike to me. You seem to want to. How am

I supposed to remember one guy? I don't stare at everybody who passes my desk. If they're not checking out a book, I may not even look at them. I'm supposed to be sorting books most of the time anyway. And I'm doing my own studying when I think I can get away with it. Between sorting and studying, I don't see half the people who come and go.'' All of that was lead-up for the one word he'd been waiting to say from the start. "Sorry.''

I thanked him and stepped into the stacks themselves. As the name implied, the basement had been divided into two floors of shelving stacked one on top of the other. The same olive drab ironwork that supported the upper floor of shelves and the catwalk aisles between the shelves also formed the uprights of the study cubicles that ran along the outside wall of the basement. From the rear partition of each cubicle hung a fixed wooden seat; from the front partition, a black rubber desktop and a single shelf. Beneath each shelf was a fluorescent light that hummed as it worked. On the side of the basement where I started, the left-hand side from Janklow's point of view, only three cubicles were lit.

I stopped at each of the three in turn and tried a variation of the pitch I'd used on Janklow. I omitted my own connection to the case, suggesting instead that I was trying to help clear a dormmate. This change in tactics was inspired by the first student I questioned, a coed who was so startled when I stepped out of the darkness that I instinctively distanced myself from the Cleveland Circle crime.

The coed hadn't been in the library on the night in question. None of the students in the left-hand cubicles had.

I started to cross the room, walking between the last shelf of books and a wire screen wall that set off a restricted area. Before I'd gotten very far, a figure stepped from the center aisle into my row, blocking my way. Detective Craney.

He waited for me to come to him. I had time as I finished my walk to kick myself for not anticipating that the police would be in Bapst, too, looking as I was for Friday night regulars.

Craney said nothing as I approached him and nothing for some time after I'd arrived. His silence was more intimidating than any tough guy remark would have been, because it took me back to my interrogation of the day before. I looked around for Kossel, my protector, and spotted Janklow, guiltily backing toward his desk.

"Wait a minute," Craney said to him. He reached to his right, locked his fingers into a wire door set in the wire wall, and rattled it. "What's through here?"

"Thesis room," Janklow said, so softly that I could barely hear him. He swallowed. "Doctoral theses."

"Who has the key?"

"I do." The librarian patted the pockets of his chinos and came up with a small key ring.

"Open it."

He did as he was told, opening the mesh door and then stepping into the darkness beyond with his hands outstretched like a sleepwalker's. He was feeling for the cord to a light, I realized a second before he found and pulled it. The light revealed shelves of thin volumes—the size if not the thickness of high school yearbooks—bound in blue or gray.

"Thanks," Craney said. "That will be all for the moment." When Janklow freed up the space, the policeman jerked his thumb toward it. "In."

I stepped into the thesis room, noting despite my rising panic that there were only six rows of shelves divided by the center aisle. The rough stone of the basement wall was just ahead of me. I reached the dangling light cord and stopped.

"Tired?" Craney asked. "Keep going."

I took another step and then felt as much as heard Craney reaching up to pull the light switch. The darkness blinded me temporarily, but that didn't halt the march. Craney pushed me forward. I felt my way with outstretched arms, as Janklow had done. The basement wall that had seemed so close took forever to reach. So long that my eyes adjusted themselves to the faint light coming in from the stacks. Even so, I didn't lower my arms. I was waiting for the policeman to push me forward against the stone.

"Turn around," he said, his voice just above a whisper.

I did, seeing his short stout silhouette, smelling his hair cream.

"What have you found?" he asked.

"Huh?"

"I know what you're doing. I've heard about you. You're the kid detective. I want to know what you've found."

My relief was dizzying. "Nothing so far," I managed to say. "I just got here."

"How about at your dorm? Don't tell me you haven't been sniffing around there."

"I don't know anything but what you've told me."

Craney took a quick step forward, backing me into the wall. "Who told you?"

"You and Detective Kossel and the first two detectives."

"When did we tell you anything?"

"The first guys told me the time of the attack. Nine-thirty. It's the time they kept asking me about. They only interviewed brown-haired men, which told me they'd found brown hairs. You confirmed that yesterday.'' I started to reach up to touch the remains of my forelock, but decided to let bygones be bygones. ''You told me whose alibis you don't like with your second round of questioning. And you told me you don't have a blood type for the rapist.''

''How?'' Craney asked, less hostile now.

''By not taking any blood samples. I don't understand that. How can there be a rape without…''

''Semen? You're a delicate flower. For your information, you can't always get a blood type from semen, even when you have some to test. We don't, because our rapist didn't leave us any. He yanked her clothes off and penetrated her, but he didn't come. He couldn't, the creep. That's why he beat her to death. He punished her for his sorry performance.''

''You couldn't get a blood type from the hairs you found?''

''No. They'd gotten caught in a ring on the victim's hand and been pulled out, but the damn rain washed them clean. Like it washed that key. Any ideas about that little item?''

I shook my head. ''It may have nothing to do with the attack.''

''We might believe that if the right person's key had turned up missing. Or if someone had had a key replaced in the last couple of weeks. But you all had your keys. Every last one of you. That means somebody scrambled to find a replacement, somebody who knew he'd lost his and where he'd lost it. He got one away from that numb-nuts Foley somehow, before we came asking about it. Of course, if it was Foley himself who lost the key, replacing it would have been simple."

He waited for me to comment, to help hang the man who'd tried to hang me.

"You've got hair samples now," I said. "You'll be comparing them."

"That won't tell us much. We don't have a magic machine to match hairs up. Most we can hope for is to narrow the field a little. What we need is somebody willing to talk. Somebody on the inside. Think about it, kid. You're with us or against us. This isn't the students versus the pigs. This is every man who won't rape a woman and beat her up against an animal who will. Do you understand that?"

"Yes," I said.

"Good. Go back to your building. That's where you can be some help. Keep your eyes open." He stuck something in my shirt pocket. "Call me if you find anything. Me, remember. Nobody else."

He stepped out of my way, and I hurried past him. "Wait a minute," he said, grabbing my arm. "When you go by that library guy, act like I gave you a hard time."

"You got it," I said.

FIFTEEN

CRANEY'S IMPLICIT ORDER was that I should limit my poking around to Two Sutherland and leave the rest of the world to the police. He seemed to be assuming that we students were all open with one another, that we might actually know who the murderer was or at least sense it, though some long-haired-kid ESP.

There *had* been a lot of loose talk and speculation, at least while Knaff had clung to life. Since her death, the talk had dried up. Three of Two Sutherland's coeds had been removed from the dorm by their parents. The rest of the population, male and female, seemed to be staying away from the place as much as possible.

For that reason alone, I had to work outside again. Besides, stepping beyond the bounds set by the police was standard practice in the paperback PI novels that had provided my training, such as it was. So I went back to checking alibis, with a shorter list to check. It was shorter because, as Craney discreetly informed me via a late-night phone call, comparison of the hair samples had eliminated two of the suspects, Cully and Riggio. I set out to eliminate five of the remaining six.

Foley's alibi, like mine, was so bad it couldn't be checked. Newcomb, the other suspect on the first floor, claimed to have been attending a showing of *Casablanca,* alone, at an art house near Copley Square. Though that story hadn't impressed the police, it seemed reasonable enough to me, because Newcomb had asked half the residents of the dorm to go along without finding any takers.

Nevertheless, I made a nuisance of myself at the movie theater, learning only that the staff had all been stoned that night and could barely account for their own whereabouts.

From film, I moved to the legitimate theater, which is to say, I next checked the story of James Courtney Murray. I waited for an afternoon when I knew Murray would be in class. Then I visited the performance space where Mary, Harry, and I had struggled through *Hamlet* late in the prior semester. The makeshift theater was in one of the older halls, Lyons, in a big room that had once been the faculty cafeteria. A square stage had been built in the center of the square space, with folding chairs on risers on all four sides. The resulting seating, though limited, was more than equal to the demand.

The double doors to the theater, each wearing an identical poster for *Measure for Measure,* were unlocked. I walked in, thinking as I had on the night of the *Hamlet* marathon that the old dining room's rededication to Shakespeare might have been suggested by certain Elizabethan cues in its interior decoration: diamond-paned windows, heavy dark beams in the ceiling, and exposed timbers in the plaster walls above a wainscoting of tile.

Near one set of windows, outside the arena formed by the risers, a woman was working at a table. She could have been a student or a junior faculty member. Her age was hard to estimate because she was overweight, so overweight that her features were distorted, her eyes narrowed, her nose and mouth miniaturized by the breadth of her face, her chin buried altogether. She was folding sheets of paper in half. Programs, I guessed. She smiled at me without interrupting her work.

"The auditions are next week," she said.

"Auditions?"

"For *Richard II.* Tuesday and Wednesday afternoons."

"I'm not here to audition."

"You're not? You have that bashful look. New recruits always have that."

"It's permanent with me. Do you know James Murray?"

Her narrow eyes widened slightly. "Yeah. Why?"

"He's in *Measure for Measure,* right?"

"That's not an answer to the question why. You're not a jealous boyfriend, are you? You don't look like one, but then Murray doesn't look like a Lothario, does he?"

"No," I said, though I wasn't sure what a Lothario was.

"How about helping me out while we're talking?" She pushed a pile of unfolded sheets my way.

I sat down across from her and began to fold the sheets widthwise. As I'd thought, they were programs for the upcoming production. Murray was listed in a catch-all collection of names at the bottom of the cast list.

"What made you think I was a jealous boyfriend?" I asked, wondering if it was too late to pass myself off as one.

"We've been waiting for you to show up. Joking about it, the members of the company. I'm the assistant director, by the way. Sally."

"Alan," I said, shaking her hand. "I thought Murray was interested in a woman in your group." He'd said her name fifty times during the fall semester. Now when I needed it, I couldn't recall it. "She played Ophelia."

"Meredith," Sally said, "our company femme fatale. She's playing Mariana in *Measure.* Frank, he's our director, always puts Meredith in our booth during the activities fair. That way we're sure to net a lot of moonstruck volunteers like Murray. If Meredith had been here, you would have auditioned fast enough. Murray followed her around like a puppy. At least for a while. When did you first begin to suspect something?''

''Suspect?''

''Between your girlfriend and Murray. Was it, say, last November? That's when we started to think that Murray was cheating on Meredith, so to speak. He stopped looking at her all the time like Antonio looks at Isabella.'' I paused in midfold, and she added, ''They're characters from our current play. And he started disappearing.''

''Murray or Antonio?''

''Murray. He played several parts in *Hamlet*. Several walk-ons. Mostly he stood with a banner in the background of the court scenes. He didn't really have to sit through all the rehearsals, but he did. So he could salivate over Meredith for the maximum amount of time. That was the first inside joke about Murray. He didn't have any lines himself, but he was here so much he had everybody else's part down by heart.''

''When did he start disappearing?'' I asked, afraid we'd wandered to a new topic.

''Around the time I'm talking about, last November, when he lost interest in Meredith. There was this gap in the play when Murray wasn't on stage. Between the play within a play in act three and Ophelia's funeral in act five.''

I remembered the gap. Harry had slept through it. ''And Murray was slipping out of rehearsals?''

''Yes. He was so clever about it, it was hilarious. He'd be sitting all by himself in the last row of the darkest part of the house. Then he'd be gone. Half an hour later, he'd be back, pretending he'd never been away. We made a game of pretending, too, pretending we hadn't missed him, which he never caught onto. He was blinded by love, no offense.''

"How long did this go on?"

"It's still going on. At least it was until a week ago Friday.''

The night of the Cleveland Circle attack. "What happened then?''

"A big blowup between Frank and Murray. It's been coming for some time. Murray's mouthy for a freshman. He's been putting down *Measure* ever since the play was announced. After *Hamlet*, nothing else is good enough for him. Frank thinks *Measure for Measure* is an important play, for the bed trick if for no other reason.''

"What's the bed trick?''

"The two female leads are switched. The bad guy, Antonio, thinks he's getting to sleep with Isabella, the virgin, but Mariana secretly takes her place. That was enough to make the play too hot for the Victorians and their spiritual descendants. It's just coming into its own now.''

"So the blowup was about artistic differences?''

"No. They were just the primer. The thing that set it off was Murray's vanishing act. None of us expected him to even sign on for another play, not after he got over Meredith. But he did. We always need warm bodies, so Frank cast him again. Murray showed up for every rehearsal, like he always did, and two or three nights a week he'd slip away.

"It wasn't so funny this semester. There isn't as big a gap in his stage time, and he was always missing his entrances. A week ago Friday, he came in half an hour late, soaking wet. When Frank called him on it, Murray went nuts. I thought they were going to duke it out right there on the stage. But Murray just stomped away. I'm surprised Frank didn't can him. He would have, if we hadn't been ready to open. You put up with temperament from actors, not from spear carriers.''

''When was he gone that evening? What time?''

''He slipped out about eight. He didn't get back until almost nine.''

''And he stormed out right after that?''

''Yeah.''

No wonder the police weren't taking Murray's alibi very seriously. They had to have talked to the members of the Shakespearean company. Which made it odd that Sally, a very savvy member, should have been so quick to misinterpret my interest in Murray.

That discrepancy was a warning to me, but I was slow on the uptake. Even when Sally looked past me and called to someone entering the room, I continued my folding.

''Thank God you finally got here,'' she said, her voice suddenly hard. ''I've been in here alone with one of them.''

I turned and saw two men enter. The first looked like a weight lifter and the second like the guy who spotted for him. ''One of them who?'' the spotter asked.

''One of those creeps from Sutherland Road. Look at his hair; it's chopped off like Murray's. And he's been asking about Murray and the night of the rape. It's been all I could do not to shake. Get him out of here.''

I stood up to demonstrate that I was capable of moving all by myself. The weight lifter wasn't impressed. He grabbed the front of my sweatshirt and pulled me toward the double doors while asking, ''Scared Sally, huh?''

I was too busy trying to get my feet under me to parry that rhetorical thrust. I danced like a marionette on the end of my escort's arm, out the doors and down the single flight of stairs to Lyons's front door. I was still off balance when Sally's protector let me go. I cleared the entrance, landing on the sidewalk outside on my hands and knees.

Two passersby helped me to my feet. "What was that, man?" one of them asked me.

"A tough audition," I said.

SIXTEEN

THAT NIGHT Mary trimmed my hair. She'd been after me to let her do it since the day the police had started the job, but I'd resisted, partly on general biblical principles, partly because of a subtle difference in our relationship.

Since the night of the attack, we'd spied on the police together, eaten our meals together, ridden the shuttle between the campus and Cleveland Circle together, but never really been together. We hadn't recaptured the illusion we'd enjoyed since Christmas, the feeling of being one, of sharing the same thoughts, of having each other's company always, even when we were physically apart. Now physical togetherness was most of what we had. We'd been close constantly, but this impromptu haircut was as personal as our proximity had gotten.

It might have been too close for Mary. She stepped away less than a minute into the preliminaries. "Unless you really let me shorten the sides, you're going to look Dutch no matter what I do. I mean, you're going to look like the kid on the Dutch Boy Paint cans. Except that he's a blond and dresses better."

She was babbling, but that was okay by me. For one thing, I found Mary's nervousness calming. "Fine," I said. "Shorten the sides. I've got two ears. I want that on the record before you start."

The operation was being performed on the glassed porch off my room. The door between the porch and the room and the one between the room and the hallway were both propped open for the sake of Mary's reputation. And so I could see Harry, my absentee roommate, from a safe distance. To insure that we could talk privately in spite of the open doors, I'd switched on Harry's radio. The Mamas and the Papas were belting one out. ''Dedicated to the One I Love.''

Mary had her own haircutting kit, a set of scissors and combs in a folding leatherette case, which inspired confidence. She undermined that confidence with her technique, which featured a great deal of combing and patting for every tentative snip. I should have steadied her with a joke or two or a monologue on some safe subject. I had other plans.

When she stepped back for the tenth time to eye the evenness of her work, I asked, ''How do you happen to know where Harry was on the night of the attack?''

I caught a second of her confused expression before she stepped up close again and resumed her combing. After that, I had to make do with her breasts as witnesses to her emotional state. I'd been conscious of them throughout the haircut, as they'd often been only inches from my nose. I noted now their rapid rise and fall, which was at odds with the calm tone Mary affected when she answered me.

''He walked me back from the campus one morning. We were both down near Higgins. It's as long a walk uphill to the shuttle stop from Higgins as it is from there down to here. I mean, it's not, but it seems as long. I like walking around the reservoir if I have someone to keep me company.''

''You weren't afraid to have him for company?''

''No. Harry?''

''You must have been thinking about the attack. You asked him where he was that night.''

''No I didn't. He just told me.''

"That he'd gone down to the combat zone?"

"Right."

"What time did he go?"

Mary had painstakingly positioned the scissors for another snip. Now she slowly drew them back. "You haven't talked to Harry?"

"No," I said.

"Why not?"

"Things haven't been the same since that night."

"I know," Mary said. Then, quickly, "He said he went down around eight-thirty. He didn't get back until almost midnight. Did he wake you coming in?"

"No. I was still awake."

"I couldn't sleep that night myself," Mary said, presenting me with a crossroads in the conversation.

I stuck to the main path. "Did he say which bar he'd gone to?"

"He couldn't remember the name. The police didn't like that. I guess he tried a couple of places before he finally got served. The bar was on Washington Street, he knew that much. The entrance was down a flight of stairs. He remembered that the wallpaper on the stairs was red.

"The police drove them down there—Harry and his father—to look for the place. Harry thought they found the right bar. The Red Garter. But nobody remembered him."

"They wouldn't admit it if they did, not to the police. They'd lose their license for serving him."

"Are you going to check out his story?"

"Yes," I said. I waited for her to ask me not to run the risk, to give up poking into the murder altogether. I wanted her to, and not just because that echo of fictional warnings delivered by fictional girlfriends to fictional detectives would have reassured me that I was still stumbling in the right direction.

"Things haven't been the same between us since that night," Mary said. "Between you and me."

"No."

"You're being too hard on yourself. We can make everything right."

"How?" I asked.

She ruffled my hair, undoing all her careful arranging in her attempt at a spontaneous gesture. "By loving one another," she said.

I DECIDED TO VISIT the bars on Washington Street on the following afternoon. The odds of encountering the bartenders and waitresses who had been on duty during Harry's alleged visit would have been better after dark, but I wanted daylight. I'd already managed to get myself thrown out of a classroom building with my questioning. There was no telling what trouble I could get into in a neighborhood called the combat zone. Not that I was honest enough to admit I was scared. I told myself that I'd probably encounter the same people at three that I would have at eight, and that, as a bonus, they'd be fresher mentally.

I rationalized my decision to take someone with me almost as desperately. I'd been wanting to confront Murray over his nonalibi, but I hadn't found the right moment. Now I was tempted by the chance to get two unpleasant jobs out of the way at the same time. At breakfast I asked Murray to go barhopping. He guessed right off that I was more interested in Harry's alibi than beer, but he signed on anyway. We arranged to meet at the Green Line trolley station across from the campus church.

Murray talked about the Red Sox during the long ride downtown. I let him, watching block after block of apartment buildings slip by and thinking how nice it would be to trade any one of them for Two Sutherland. My bodyguard quieted when the trolley slipped underground at Kenmore Square, becoming a subway train. It was my chance to mention his rehearsal disappearances, but I was too busy studying the tunnel wall that charged our window or retreated as the old car lurched and swayed.

In the end, it was Murray who brought the subject up. We emerged from the catacombs at the Boylston Street station on the edge of the Common and headed away from the park, toward Washington Street. I spotted the Red Garter as soon as we got to Washington, but I decided to save it for last. We started with the bar closest to the subway stop on the theory that Harry would have, too. Two of the first three bars we tried served us without asking for identification, which was better luck than Harry claimed to have had. But none of the help recognized Harry from the picture I showed them, a group shot of Harry and his parents on a grassy Cape Cod dune, which I'd borrowed from our room. The excuses were consistent: Boston was full of thirsty college kids and we all looked alike.

We were lingering over our beers in the third bar when Murray said, "You checked up on me yet, Keane?"

"Yes," I said.

"What did you find out?"

"That you really don't have an alibi. You skipped out of your rehearsal that night in plenty of time to get back to Cleveland Circle by nine-thirty. Where did you go?"

"I walked around in the rain, like you. Too bad we didn't bump into one another. Know why I skipped?"

"You got into a fight with the director." I could have

left it at that, but my two beers had gone straight to my head. "You'd slipped away from the rehearsal earlier that night. Why did you do it? Was it for a girl?"

"A girl?" Murray repeated and laughed. "For love, you mean? Love is the slowest form of suicide known to man, Keane. Shooting yourself in the foot is a faster way to end it all, and in the long run much less painful."

"Never thought I'd miss the Shakespeare," I said.

"Fuck you," Murray said, bringing his bottle down hard on the bar. "What was your plan here, Sherlock? Were you going to get me drunk enough to tell you the story of my life? If so, you'd better switch to Seven-up. You're already so far ahead of me I could play you like a pipe. I could have you describing the size and shape of the fair Fitz's left nipple.

"Don't get sore, Keane. I'm just trying to understand you. And while we're on the subject of Fitz, why don't you get her out of that building? I would, if I were nuts about her. She isn't safe."

"You think one of us did it?"

"Don't you? Don't tell me you're just trying to clear us all. You can't clear everybody, Keane. Not in this life. You can't make things right for everybody. Somebody's got to end up being guilty. You'd better learn to face that or find yourself another hobby. In the meantime, find yourself another sidekick." He stood up.

"There's one more bar to hit," I said.

"Hit it yourself. If it hits you back, I'll mail your things to Jersey."

I argued with him as far as the sidewalk. He left me there with one last quote from *Hamlet,* which I'd asked for, more or less. He was smiling again as he delivered the line with outstretched arms to the whole block. "'We know what we are, but not what we may be.'"

I waited by the entrance to the Red Garter until Murray was out of sight, hoping he'd change his mind and come back. He didn't. I went through the front door alone and down a flight of stairs whose walls were papered in red. Keane's descent into hell, I thought. There were repeating pictures on the wallpaper, dice and roulette wheels and poker hands, every one a full house. Recorded music was coming from the room at the bottom of the stairs, "Sweet Soul Music," played loudly enough to drown out a crowd of a hundred. Most of it was being wasted, as only two of the tables in the large room were occupied and those two by couples. Affectionate couples.

I was the only customer at the bar. Even so, it took the bartender five minutes to notice me. He was heavyset, with a mustache that made Harry's look like a weekend fling, black matted hair that Mary could have spent months sorting out, and eyes that were sleepy and unfriendly at the same time.

I ordered yet another beer. When my host brought it, I had the Ohlman family portrait on the bar. "Don't like to drink alone?" he asked in an accent that might have been Portuguese. And then, before I could make any use of the opening, "Three dollars."

He waited for me to tell him it was highway robbery, but I was used to the prices on Washington Street. I placed a ten-dollar bill on the bar, and he snatched it up.

He came back and laid my change next to Harry's picture. Two dollar bills.

"I gave you a ten," I said.

"You gave me a five."

"It was a ten."

"Are you calling me a liar?"

I hadn't had that much to drink. Or maybe I had. I was suddenly struck by a new idea. The bartender had glanced at the photograph again as he'd set down my change. I decided that he knew why I was there, that he expected payment for his information, and that he'd helped himself to it. I nudged the photo his way. "Have you seen that guy before?"

"I've seen both those guys, the old one and the young one. They were here with the police. The broad I haven't seen before. She's too old for me."

"You saw the young guy twice. The first time was a week ago last Friday night. He was in here by himself."

"They asked me that, too, the police. I told them no."

"You can tell me the truth."

"You're calling me a liar again," the bartender pointed out.

"I understand why you couldn't talk in front of the police. Harry, the young guy, is underage. You couldn't admit serving an underage kid."

"We don't serve underage kids."

"You served me," I said helpfully. "I'm underage."

I'd called him a liar for the third time in as many minutes. It might have been a new Red Garter record.

"If you're not out of here by the time I get around this bar, I'll boot your skinny ass up to daylight."

He reached out then, not for me, but to grab something from the bar top. I grabbed, too. We were grabbing for different things, luckily, so there was no contact. I was after the Ohlman family photo. The bartender seized my two dollars.

"My tip, dickhead," he said, by way of thanks. Then he lumbered toward the open end of the bar. Long before he reached it, I was on the stairs and climbing. I waited until I was safely on the sidewalk again before I gave into laughing at myself from relief.

I was still smiling when I reached the edge of the Com-

mon and the granite mausoleum that sheltered the stairs
to the Green Line. Harry Ohlman was guarding the entrance. I could have turned away before he spotted me,
doubled back to the Arlington Street entrance, and eluded
him entirely. I kept going. As I did I thought, she told
him I'd be here. Mary.

There was time as I finished my walk for me to admire
Harry's strategy. He would have run the risk of missing
me if he'd tried to search the combat zone. So he'd staked
out the subway entrance, knowing I'd pass there sooner
or later. I was close enough to smell the pigeon droppings
on the little building's glass roof before Harry addressed
me.

"We have to talk." Like me he was dressed for the
unseasonably balmy weather, in his case in a blue work
shirt and jeans. The park was dotted with individuals,
couples, and small groups enjoying the perfect day, but
the crowd was nothing like it would have been on a Saturday or a Sunday. Harry didn't have to lead me far along
the asphalt path before we found a private stretch. He
swung around at me then and forced me off the pavement
and onto the grass.

"Stay the hell out of my business," he said. "Play
detective with your own neck." He spotted the photograph in my shirt pocket and ripped it out. "And keep
your hands off my stuff."

"I'm trying to help."

He didn't believe me any more than Murray had, but
his reaction was more personal. "I don't want your help.
If I was sitting in the electric chair, I wouldn't want your
help." His anger was also a reminder of Murray, Harry's
a prolonged rumble to Murray's lightning flash. Just then
I had a lightning flash of my own, but not of anger.

"Mary didn't tell you I'd be checking your story today,'' I said. "She didn't know when I'd be down here. Murray told you." The deduction had me smiling again, though it was a good time not to be.

Harry's blow was a right, as I later reconstructed events. I never actually saw the punch coming. I was grinning at him one moment. The next I was staring up at a clear blue sky.

SEVENTEEN

THAT RIGHT CROSS marked the low point of my relationship with Harry, at least during our college years. It was also very nearly the end of my investigation of Francine Knaff's murder. The police kept at it—Detective Craney threatened me weekly for a time—but they never made an arrest. March turned to April and April to May and our freshman year ended.

With it ended Cleveland Circle's time as a home for freshmen and transfers. Word about the off-campus accommodations had spread and then some. In the housing lottery for the upcoming year, all the old apartments were snapped up by upperclassmen, even the fragmented flats of Two Sutherland. Harry and Mary and Murray and I were all tossed into the dormitory ghetto, for a year at least.

Unexpectedly, Harry and I landed together. He surprised me just before the lottery by asking if I wanted to remain roommates. I surprised us both by saying yes. I decided later that Mary had worked out the truce, negotiating behind the scenes. The truth was probably subtler. She and I were almost as close again at the end of the semester as we'd been before the murder. Harry, who was now openly stuck on Mary, may have clung to me as a way of staying in touch with her.

I'd been so certain I'd need a new roommate that I'd approached Alan Avery at the last minute to see if he'd be interested. We were doing laundry at the same time one evening in the crowded laundromat across the street from Two Sutherland. Though Avery hadn't asked me to, I was holding a dryer for him, feeding in dimes until my sheets began to brown. While we were waiting for his washer to spin itself out, I asked him.

"Thanks for the invitation, Keane. But I can't help you out. You might ask Pete," he added, naming his own roommate. "He's looking for somebody. The thing is, I'm leaving Boston College."

"Why?" I asked.

He shrugged. "It's what I do. Let me move this stuff over to your dryer and we can step outside. I'm losing weight in here."

Outside it was almost dark, but there was still blue in the sky if you looked high enough. A dark blue touched with early stars. The hum of traffic came up to us from the circle, the sound as steady and as easily tuned out as surf at the shore. I gave Avery a Parliament from my own pack. He lit us up with his Zippo and handed it to me.

"A going-away present," he said. "Some lucky souls are leaving already, I noticed. The ones with their exams behind them. Your folks coming to pick you up?"

"No," I said, "I'm taking the bus."

"What about your books?"

"Taking the bus, too. I sent the first box today."

I started to ask him where he'd go, whether his parents' divorce had left him a place to go. I didn't ask, but he was thinking of it all the same.

"I've been down on myself for telling you about my folks, Keane. I was feeling sorry for you that day because I thought the cops were going to tear into you. I've been sure you'd spill it to somebody, but I never got any grief or any phony sympathy, so I know you didn't. Thanks."

"No problem," I said.

Avery scratched at one of his coarse eyebrows with his thumbnail, producing a sound I could hear above the traffic. He looked all in, but then finals had done that to most of us.

"The reward for keeping a secret is another secret. You never asked me about the falling-out I had with my parents. Not in words, anyway. You've got a way of asking without asking, which is an interesting talent. You remember me mentioning the shit fight?"

"Yes," I said.

"It was over my old school. The one I left to come here. I'm sure you read that much between the lines. It was Mount Saint Mary's. You've heard of it, right? Good school. The Maryknoll Fathers run it. They're quite a different crew from our Jesuits. Once upon a time, Mount Saint Mary's turned out a lot of Maryknoll priests. It still turns out a few every year. I thought I was going to be one of them."

"A priest?"

"Yeah. Big surprise, right? You're thinking about my lady friends. I guess I have overdone that a little bit. Sex wasn't the reason I dropped out, but it was one of the things I turned to as compensation for all I'd given up."

"What was the reason?"

"Keane to the heart of the mystery!" Avery said and flicked his cigarette toward the now black sky. He watched its fiery arc and said, "There never is one reason, Keane. Not for a choice that big. No single truth that explains any of us. That's what I tried to tell you that day we walked up Beacon. Not that I haven't looked hard for an explanation. An excuse. I told my parents it had always been their dream and not mine, but that wasn't true. I'd dreamed of it plenty, but not the same way they did. Not for the honor or the prestige. I saw it as a way of getting to the center, the dark dense core of things. A way of getting off the plastic surface where most people live their lives.''

"But it didn't turn out that way?"

"Who knows? I was years away from finding out when I quit. The only thing I learned was that I wasn't up to the challenge, that I was a born surface dweller who only thought he wanted more. What I really want is the empty, Motorola, American Express, General Motors life I'd bugged my parents for living. The kind of life they don't want themselves all of a sudden, which is the ultimate double cross.''

Not far from where we were standing, a station wagon with New York plates was double parked. As we watched, Tregnab emerged from Two Sutherland carrying one end of a foot locker. The other end was being carried by a shorter, broader version of Tregnab, who must have been his brother. When they'd gotten the locker stowed, Tregnab crossed the street and pumped our hands.

"It was a great year," he said. "A hellacious year!"

"I guess that depends on how you define hell," Avery said when the station wagon had freed up the street. "Watch out for that guy at class reunions. He'll be hugging everybody." We listened to the traffic surf. Then he said, "How about you, Keane?"

"I doubt I'll make any reunions."

"Sorry. I was doubling back to an earlier topic. Are you a surface dweller or do you want more?"

I shrugged. Lately even the surface had felt dangerous to me, but I didn't want to admit that to Avery.

We'd been standing shoulder to shoulder at the curb. Now Avery turned to face me, obliging me to turn toward him. I almost stepped backward, intimidated by his boxer's stance.

"If you're just playing a game with this questioning routine of yours," he said, "fine. God knows most people are playing games most of the time. And playing parts all the time. But if you're really serious about knowing the answers, it means giving your life to the search. *Think* about that. *Think, period.*"

I WAS STILL SEATED at the bar in the Last Stand when Harry found me. He was unduly smug about that modest feat. "I thought you might be here when you weren't in the suite. What number is that?" he asked, pointing to the beer before me.

"One," I said. "The loneliest number."

Harry looked to the bartender, a recent fine arts graduate, for confirmation. The youngster nodded glumly. "Bring him one with a head on it," Harry said. "And the same for me."

He looked like he needed coffee more than alcohol. "Your lunch didn't go well?"

"It wasn't cheering, Owen, let me put it that way. Rita's in a tough spot. And she's really worried about her daughter."

"She has good reason to be." I described my surprise lunch with Melanie. "She never heard her father mention Phyllis Garrity, by the way."

"Rita never heard of her either. Guess it's been a wasted day so far."

"Yes and no," I said. I came clean then regarding my unauthorized approach to Wayne Woodson. Harry listened to my confession with the stoicism of long experience. Afterward he wanted to discuss Woodson's almost defiant attitude, but my mind wandered back to

Melanie Murray. Thinking of her in the context of my visit to Woodson's office led me to a small discovery.

"What?" Harry asked when he noticed my inattention.

"Nothing. I was just thinking that Melanie looks a little like Bergen, Woodson and Garrity's daughter. I saw an old picture of Bergen in Woodson's office."

"That's not too surprising, Owen. Woodson looks a little like Murray. I was struck by that yesterday when Koie Mustafa showed us his picture. Same big eyes, same dark coloring, same beak of a nose. Besides, all kids tend to look alike these days. They try to look alike. And sound alike. I hate it when Amanda sounds like she came from southern California. She's never even been to southern California. How does that happen?"

"It's in their jeans," I said, but Harry didn't get it.

"Speaking of Mustafa, she's expecting me to stop by to hear the results of the famous audit. Drink up."

EIGHTEEN

KOIE MUSTAFA WAS thrilled to see Harry. She was less emotionally involved in my reappearance. In fact, she seemed to have forgotten me. I felt almost as flat toward her, until she did something to earn my thanks forever. On the doorstep of the Office of Alumni Oversight and Coordination conference room, with the auditors and their stacks of computer printout just beyond, Mustafa paused and tapped her head, the universal gesture for dawning light. She handed Harry her plastic mug and dug into her ever-present folder of papers.

"I almost forgot. I was able to get you a copy of James Murray's undergraduate transcript. I walked over to the registrar's office this morning and stood there until they printed it out for me. They pretend these things take days, like they used to years ago. But we all have computers now. We all know the job's just two keystrokes and a lot of sitting around looking busy. With me standing there, they had to skip the second part."

She started to hand the single sheet to Harry, but I snatched it. "I'd better get on this right away." I didn't add "boss" or "sir," but I managed to convey the sense of both.

Mustafa nodded approvingly. As I'd hoped, she found it fitting that her hero had energetic minions. The hero himself was less pleased, but he let me go with his own nod, a solemn bow as he turned to his fate.

I wasted no time quitting Burke Hall, even though it was spitting snow outside. I crossed College Road and

reentered the campus proper before sitting down on a
stone bench to study the transcript.

The complete history of Murray's four years at Boston
College was reproduced on a single sheet of paper. In
part, that trick had been worked through the use of an
extremely small typeface. But the report's designers had
also omitted information. They'd given me a number and
an abbreviated title for every course Murray had taken,
the department that had offered it, the credit hours, and
a code that told me whether the course had been a core
requisite, a major requisite, or an elective. Finally, the
single-line entry per course gave me Murray's grade. Despite his early drinking, he'd started well, with As and
Bs during the first semester of our freshman year. Things
had gone downhill from there. Not that I was interested
in Murray's grade point average. I wanted the names of
his instructors, and those weren't listed on the transcript.

By then I was half frozen in a sensitive area. I gave
up my stone seat and walked to the college's new library,
the Thomas P. O'Neil Library, which had replaced an old
parking lot. The new building lacked Bapst's classic architecture, being boxy with few windows, but the style
deficiencies were made up for with interior space. Beyond security gates that were duplicates of the ones Harry
and I had seen at the Boston Public Library was a carpeted area at least twice as large as was needed for the
shelves of books and randomly spaced study cubicles.
Bapst must have seemed as spacious once, I thought, but
the scribblers of the world had managed to fill it.

I lucked onto a librarian who saw my request for old
course catalogs as an interesting challenge. We tracked
them down together on a floor the young woman referred
to as "the stacks." The name was a nod to college tra-
dition and not a description of the basement, which was

as roomy and almost as well lit as the entrance level. I ended up safely tucked in at a white-walled study desk with eight course catalogs, one for each of Murray's eight semesters at BC.

They were also my old semesters, my old catalogs. As was usual for me, I approached the task at hand circumspectly, paging through the booklets at random, looking for classes I'd taken myself. I found a few, but missed many more, which added to the feeling of unreality the whole library-of-the-future experience was giving me. More familiar and reassuring than the cryptic course names were the graffiti written on the interior walls of my little cubicle. A competition to define the word love seemed to have inspired most of the ballpoint notations, which included the poetic: "Love is a mutual rising," the flippant: "Love is a byproduct of the brewing process," and the cynical: "Love is a registered trademark of the Hallmark Corporation."

I eventually got down to work, looking up every psychology course Murray had taken—three in four years—and checking to see if any of these had been taught by Phyllis Garrity. None of them had. I then checked Murray's English courses, looking for Wayne Woodson's name, and drew an identical blank. I sat and listened to the electrons colliding in the light fixture above me and thought it over. Then I flipped back through the catalogs that contained the entries for Murray's three psych courses and wrote down the name of the instructor listed for each.

While I had my pen out, I leaned into the cubicle and left an addendum to the "Love is..." competition: "Love is the slowest form of suicide known to man." I signed it JCM.

On my way out of O'Neil, I tracked down my original

library assistant to thank her and to ask where I'd find the Office of Graduate Studies. It was in nearby Gasson Hall, the oldest building on campus and, for my money, the finest. For many local people Gasson's slender-spired clock tower was the dominant symbol of the college, as it could be seen from as far away as the reservoir. Harry had done an oil painting of the tower once with the water as foreground. It had hung in his law office back in the lost days when I'd worked for him. He'd made the hall look dark and even sinister, which is how it appeared to me now, with March snow swirling down out of a ragged sky.

They'd probably renovated Gasson two or three times since I'd been a student, but there was only so much they could do with the sagging stone floors and the dark medieval woodwork. Against that background, the fresh paint and wallpaper looked no more permanent than the St. Patrick's Day decorations that were stapled to the bulletin board of the office where I eventually came to rest.

I found myself standing across a counter from a stout man with a goatee that looked as out of place on his broad Irish face as a monocle would have. The face was also pink, which might have been a reaction to the weather, and friendly, which I hoped was a reaction to seeing another Irish face, a narrow dark one. Mine.

"I'm told you can get just about any information out of a computer these days with a couple of keystrokes," I said.

"Who told you that?" the goateed man asked.

"Koie Mustafa, Director of the OAOC. The Office of Alumni Oversight and Coordination," I explained, adopting Mustafa's self-importance as part of my disguise. "I'm writing an article for her on Dr. Phyllis Garrity. For the *Alumni Report*."

"I've heard of her."

"Of Director Mustafa or Dr. Garrity?"

"The doctor. I think I have."

"That's the problem we're having. People *think* they've heard of her. The name is familiar. But not everyone is sure what she does. Not everyone knows that she is a nationally recognized authority on the psychology of rape. It's more than a problem. It's an injustice."

"What can I do to help?"

"I'm trying to compile a complete list of Dr. Garrity's teaching assignments for the college. A complete list. It's never been done before. We're even looking into her work as a graduate assistant, which is where you come in."

I consulted Murray's transcript and bet everything on a single roll of the dice. "We have reason to believe that she worked as an assistant to Professor Joshua Ackles in 1968 on a survey course called Aspects of Modern Psychology. Could you confirm that?"

"Professor Garrity doesn't remember?"

I was shocked, though mildly. "I can't waste my interview time with background questions. Not with a woman of her standing. I have to have it all down cold when I go in. Can you call up the information for me? Is it two keystrokes or was Director Mustafa underestimating the challenge?"

"People who never use computers tend to," he said, leaving me to guess whether he meant Mustafa or me. "I'm not sure those files were even converted when we went from mainframe to distributed processing. But I'll give it a shot. Have a seat."

I sat down on an armless sofa and paged through a copy of the very magazine I was pretending to represent, the *Alumni Report*. It was the issue I'd already examined, number one of the current volume. I located Wayne Woodson's picture and studied it. Harry had been right, up to a point. Woodson and Murray did share some common features. I'd missed the resemblance, my mental image of Murray having gotten fuzzy over time. Another problem was Woodson's habitual expression, which was like nothing I could picture from Murray. It was the expression of a man who was absolutely certain of his answers. Given Woodson's radical academic specialty, it might have been more correct to say it was the look of a man who was sure there were no answers.

A counterargument arrived at that moment, a tiny answer delivered by a stout computer jockey in a goatee. "Guess I owe your director an apology," he said. "I found it right away. Phyllis Garrity worked as an assistant to Professor Ackles from 1968 to 1970. Their first class together was the one you asked about. Aspects of Modern Psychology."

NINETEEN

I STOPPED BACK by the OAOC offices to see how the audit meeting was going and found that it was already breaking up. I was a little disappointed. I'd pictured it dragging on for days, with Mustafa's secretary, Imogene, and I slipping food under the conference room door at irregular intervals.

Harry and I drove back to the hotel together, exchanging brief reports en route. The preliminary audit had gone as we'd expected. James Murray, though no financial genius, had been a competent and honest treasurer. Not a penny of the Friends of the Eagle's funds was missing. Despite that, Harry had suggested several additions and changes to the auditors' final report, as a way of stretching our already strained reason for being in Boston.

As we presented the Lexus to the Dominion's valet, Harry congratulated me on establishing a 1968 link between Murray and Garrity, without quibbling about how flimsy that link was. He was tired, though by my reckoning, he'd had an easy day.

The quibbling came later, during dinner in the Dominion's first-class restaurant, the Raj. Harry had spent an hour or so after our return soaking his leg and napping in his whirlpool tub, which had brought him back to life. I'd wasted the same hour watching a spring training report on ESPN, so I wasn't nearly as peppy. While I chewed on the grilled quail I'd mistakenly ordered, Harry listed his doubts. Murray being in a class Garrity had helped with might be a coincidence. She couldn't be expected to remember every student she'd taught last year, never mind twenty-seven years ago. So her claim never to have met Murray could not be dismissed as a lie.

I tossed the bone I'd been gnawing onto my bread plate. The bone was only the size of a fountain pen cartridge, but it appeared to be the best a quail could do. "We know Garrity lied to us about not knowing Murray," I said. "She tested his DNA, remember."

Harry wouldn't let me slip that one past him. "We haven't established that, Owen." He caught our waiter's eye and asked to see the cigar selection. I went back to my gnawing with some urgency as Harry added, "We'll never establish that if we can't locate the lab."

THE DNA LAB located us the next day, or so it seemed to me. I was unused to having my legwork done for me, but not Harry. When the call came in from the local Ohlman law firm after breakfast, informing us that we had a one o'clock appointment with Seetak Laboratories in nearby Quincy, Harry saw it as the planets moving in their courses.

"Things are finally breaking our way, Owen. Seetak is a lab the Ohlman firm has used on occasion. The Boston firm, I should say. We'll be representing the New York firm, my firm. Our official reason for visiting is to evaluate Seetak as a possible replacement for the Connecticut lab we've been using. The Seetak people are aware of our interest in the job they did for Garrity, but they say they can't discuss another client's work with us."

"Why are we bothering to go down there, then? Why don't we call in your cousin the policeman?"

"We'll lose control of this if Harry gets involved too soon. Seetak wants my business. And more of my Boston relations' business. They'll find a way to tell us what we want to know.''

Since the lab had admitted working for Garrity as a first step in refusing to tell us about it, it had already told me all I needed to know. But I went along for the ride, to pacify Harry and to get away from the one place on earth where Melanie Murray could find me. It was a day for a ride in any case, yesterday's snow flurries having given way to sunshine.

Quincy was a town I remembered only as a built-up area Mary and I had driven through on our way to Nantasket Beach. Harry took our old route: downtown on the Mass. Turnpike and then out again on the Southeast Expressway, which was now also called I-93. He barely had time to violate the speed limit on the outbound leg before he was breaking for Quincy's Staunton Road exit.

Like so much of Massachusetts, Quincy appeared to have bet its future on high-tech industries. Seetak was in a beautifully landscaped industrial park whose tenants all had Laboratory or Computer or Research as part of their names. The buildings were also high-tech—one of them a burnished copper cube with no visible windows. The single exception was the building we were after. Seetak occupied a pillared brick colonial that could have been the home office of a Midwestern insurance company.

''Ye olde DNA lab,'' Harry muttered as we entered.

We were greeted by a delegation of two, a tall impeccably dressed member of Harry's spiritual fraternity, the up and comers, and a woman, average in height and indifferently dressed, but sincerely friendly. The man, John Eskew, was the owner of Seetak. As soon as he heard that my last name wasn't Ohlman, he lost interest in me. He suggested to Harry that his associate, Dr. Wiese, show me around the facility while the two of them conferred.

While he slipped Harry the secret results of Garrity's test, I decided Eskew really meant.

So did Harry. He gave me a smug smile and passed me to the doctor, saying, "Owen would love to hear all the details of DNA fingerprinting."

Dr. Wiese's unsmug smile was the same one with which she'd greeted us. Above it her thin face was nearly all lively eyes. Brown eyes that looked out through big square glasses supported by a small and bony nose. Her untidy hair was brown, too. A natural brown, I decided, guessing her age to be roughly Rita Murray's thirty-five and a quarter. Her smiling lips were thin and beginning to curl at the ends, though I had yet to make my first uninformed remark.

"So," she began. "Are you a lawyer, Mr. Keane?"

"No," I said.

She wore an open light-gray lab coat with Seetak's name on it over a charcoal gray dress of straight simple lines. "But you're connected with Mr. Ohlman's firm."

"No again. I'm just along for the ride."

She didn't believe me. As she led me down a corridor, an interior corridor but one with windows, she asked, "Have you some connection with Boston College?"

My stride became even less rhythmic than usual. Wiese was better informed regarding our business than I'd guessed.

"Yes," I said. "The college and I have a connection." One they'd probably pay me to forget. I affected interest in the view through the nearest hallway window, though it only featured a technician in another gray lab coat seated at a boxy machine that could have been anything from a color copier to a nuclear bomb.

"What's your academic discipline?"

"English," I said. And then, because that sounded inadequate in the sci fi environment of the lab: "Literary deconstruction, actually."

"Deconstruction? Really? You're one of those guys who pull apart *Little Women* and put it back together as *Pretty Woman?* Who find new meanings in old texts?"

For the two or three thousandth time, I told myself to count to ten before snatching at a disguise. "It might be more correct to say we find no meaning." I tried to remember how Woodson had put it, coming up with his words, if not his magisterial tone. "Deconstruction is a challenge to the assumption that literary texts possess meaning." I added my own gloss, a secret fear that headed my list of secret fears. "Ultimately, there may be no meaning, no truth."

"We're on opposite sides of that issue," Wiese said, serious for the first time in our brief acquaintance. "Here at Seetak, we're in the business of finding truth. And, in a broader sense, those working in my field, DNA mapping, are finding meaning in everything. In every living text."

We'd come to a stop at a door that bore Dr. Wiese's full name. Rebecca Y. Wiese.

"Y?" I said before I could check the impulse.

"That's what I've always asked," she replied, her smile back and curling beautifully. "Come in. Sit down a minute. We'll chat."

The office was large but sterile, a classroom as much as a personal space, the walls decorated—if you could call it that—with poster-size diagrams. The chart nearest my chair showed rows of boxes, each box containing what appeared to be pairs of noodles.

"So you're interested in DNA fingerprinting," Wiese said, repeating Harry's assertion. It had been his way of getting back at me for skipping yesterday's audit. I nodded anyway.

The scientist looked even more businesslike behind her desk. I scanned it for something personal, a souvenir paperweight or family photo I might use to distract her, but there weren't even bite marks on her pencils.

"How much do you know about DNA?" she asked.

"Deoxyribonucleic acid."

"Yes. What do you know about it?"

"That's it."

"Come on now. You know that DNA is the genetic code for all life, from viruses on up to the Keane family. And you've heard of the famous double helix, haven't you? The twisted ladder structure of the DNA module? The uprights of the ladder are sequences of phosphate and sugar. The rungs are one of two kinds of purines in combination with one of two kinds of pyrimidines."

"That's a lot of detail," I said. "Could you keep it more general?"

"You want a higher level summary? Okay. DNA is a sequence of information that consists of four possible code combinations, called base pairs, repeated over and over. One DNA molecule contains about three million base pairs, three million iterations of the four possible code combinations."

"Higher," I said.

"Each human being has forty-six chromosomes made of DNA." She pointed to the noodle chart. "The chromosomes carry about one hundred thousand genes, a gene being a sequence of DNA that has a specific influence on the human phenotype."

"Higher."

"Higher?" Wiese sighed. "Once upon a time there

was a beautiful princess genome and a handsome prince genome.''

I started to laugh and she did, too, leaning back in her chair and tossing one of her unchewed pencils in my direction. It rolled to a stop well short of my edge of the desk.

"I thought you were interested in this," she said.

"I'm interested in your results, not in the nuts and bolts." An analogy someone had once used on me came to mind. "Say I'm a baseball fan. I know it's ninety feet between the bases, but I don't really need to know that. I certainly don't need to know why it's ninety. I just want the score of last night's game."

"Fascinating," Wiese said. "I would have guessed you were a man who lived and died over whys. It must be that we all have our own set of life-and-death whys. Everyone else's are just static on the radio." She leaned forward again. "So if I told you that we get our results by boiling samples in dog urine and spreading the goo on moldy bread during a full moon, that would be enough for you?"

"Throw in a couple of references to the Internet, and I'll buy stock in your company."

The doctor shook her head. "That's not good enough, Mr. No-meaning-deconstructionist. Listen for five minutes without interrupting. As a favor. Okay?"

"Okay."

"A complete set of human DNA is called the human genome, the recipe for a human being. No two recipes are exactly alike—except in the case of identical twins—which is why no two human beings are exactly alike. But the differences are small. For example, we all have eyes, but the color and shape vary. That's true across all parts of the human genome that we've been able to map. Only very minor variations, called alleles, occur. But there are parts of the recipe we can't decipher, parts with no function we can identify. It's as though the recipe you're reading in English suddenly shifts to Chinese for a page or two and then jumps back to English.

"These mystery sections, or polymorphic regions as they're sometimes called, appear on each of your chromosomes. And within these regions, there are tremendous variations between individuals. Especially in size—how many pages of Chinese there are before the English picks up again. The first type of DNA fingerprinting was made possible by the size variations in these mystery sections of DNA.

"We can cut up a DNA sample at specific places, the same places for every person. If it weren't for the mystery DNA, the sections we get after we make our cuts would be the same size for every individual. But the polymorphic regions make the sections different sizes for every person. When we deposit the DNA on a gel and introduce an electrical attraction, the DNA sections move toward the attraction. But the heavy ones don't move as far as the light ones. Your sections would travel a different distance than mine, because the amount of mystery DNA in your slices is different than mine.

"I won't bore you with how we fix the positions of the DNA sequences spread out on the gel by transferring them to a nylon membrane or identify them using radioactive probes or how we create autoradiographs by exposing X-ray film to the radioactively enhanced sample. The resulting picture shows the DNA sequences as little lines standing side by side in a row, something like the bar codes they use to scan groceries. The spacing of the lines depends upon the amount of mystery DNA contained in each sequence. No two people's bar codes will be the same. So if we compare a sample of your blood with blood taken from a crime scene, we can say whether or not you did the bleeding.''

''Could you use some other genetic sample? A hair, for instance?'' I asked casually.

''We can extract DNA from a hair, if it has an intact root, but the test I've just described would require a dozen or more hairs. However, a new test recently became available that works well with very tiny DNA samples. A single hair. Or the cells you leave on an envelope when you lick the flap. It even works with old or damaged DNA.''

Harry Gilder had mentioned a new test. ''Is this technique faster than the old one?''

''Yes, now that you mention it. The original test took six to eight weeks. We can perform the new one in as little as a week. It's called the polymerase chain reaction, or PCR test. Basically it uses an enzymatic process to isolate and duplicate a specific area of the DNA. We end up with billions of identical strands, a sample large enough to test. We then identify the alleles, or variations, in the sample by dipping it into a solution of probes that bind with the specific alleles we're looking for, should they be present. A dot appears on the DNA-bearing membrane when an allele is identified. By comparing the dots of an individual's sample with those of a forensic sample, we can determine whether there's a match.''

She looked at me for a time, but without her usual questioning expression. Then she reached into her desk and pulled out a manila folder. She slid it toward me. ''Here's a case that illustrates that technique, chosen entirely at random. The samples supplied consisted of exactly two human hairs, neither of them very fresh. DNA

has been extracted from Egyptian mummies, though, so
the age of these samples wasn't a problem.''

I picked up the folder. The sticker on its tab said
GARRITY. Harry wasn't being slipped the confidential
results of the tests the professor had ordered. I was. And
by Dr. Wiese. I looked up at her over the unopened
folder, wondering how she felt about Eskew's willingness
to violate a confidence for a promise of new business.
''An illustration isn't really necessary,'' I said.

''Would it help you to understand things a little better?''

''It might.''

''Then you're welcome to it.''

I opened the file and flipped through several single-
spaced pages, looking for a summary. I found it on the
last sheet. ''Sample A does not match Sample B.''

Everything we'd guessed so far was true. Garrity had
obtained hair samples from the police evidence file.
She'd had a DNA test performed. But for one suspect
only. James Courtney Murray. Nothing in Wiese's charts
and graphs was going to tell me why Garrity had singled
him out.

Wiese had stood and walked around to me. I stood,
too, and handed her the folder. ''Thank you,'' I said.

''Answer your questions?''

''Some of them.''

''I'll walk you out.''

She didn't speak as we retraced our route along the
interior corridor. I found that uncomfortable for some reason, so I hunted around for a topic to fill the void. ''Those
unexplained stretches of DNA. The polymorphic regions.''

''Yes,'' Wiese said. ''What about them?''

''What do you think they're for?''

She'd lost the urge to lecture. "They're probably just more meaningless text in a world of meaningless text."

I suddenly wished I'd handed the folder back unopened. "You don't believe that," I said. "So what's your theory?"

"Maybe they're the code for the whys we each ask. For those personal curiosities and obsessions we discussed earlier, the ones that are just static on the radio to everybody else. Or maybe they're not questions. Maybe they're answers to the questions. The big questions. Explanations hidden away by whoever or whatever put us here."

"They can't be answers," I said. "They're all different."

"You don't think the history of mankind is a pretty good indication that the answers would all be different?" Wiese asked, the twinkle alive again in her lively eyes.

I was so relieved to see it that I didn't let her question bother me. We'd arrived in the big colonial reception area. Harry and Eskew weren't there.

Wiese addressed a lonely receptionist. "Doug, please let John know that we've finished our tour."

While Doug placed the call, we walked toward the front doors and the rack where I'd left my fancy new coat. As I slipped it on, Wiese asked, "How long will you be staying in the Boston area, Mr. Keane?"

"Call me Owen," I said, though it was late in the day to be making that offer. Or so I thought. "I'm not sure how long we'll be here."

"Perhaps before you leave there'll be time for us to continue our discussion. Owen. Over dinner?"

"I'd like that."

"Rebecca?"

"Rebecca."

"Good. I'll wait for your call."

TWENTY

HARRY AND JOHN ESKEW had managed to work a drink into their meeting. Maybe two or three drinks. That reconciled Harry to my having been the recipient of the vital clue. He was reconciled in general. Almost mellow. He handed me the car keys for the drive back to Boston, which saved me the trouble of getting them away from him. As we headed north, I passed on the relevant parts of all I'd learned from Rebecca Wiese. That is, I tried to.

I'd forgotten how aggressive Boston drivers were. It all came back to me, including an old observation of Mary's to the effect that the automobile had been the unintended antidote for generations of repressed Puritan behavior. I was working so hard at keeping empty air on all four sides of the Lexus that my report came out sketchy and disjointed. It galvanized Harry into action nonetheless.

"Drive us down to Government Center, Owen. It's time we talked to Harry Gilder."

"You were afraid of losing control of the investigation last night. You're not now?"

It was a silly question. Harry wasn't afraid of anything at the moment, including lions and tigers. "This'll just be a strategy session. It's time someone really talked with Dr. Garrity."

I agreed, but I didn't think either Harry was the man for the job. "I'm not up for a strategy session," I said. "I'll drop you and the car off and take the trolley back to Chestnut Hill."

"Keep the car. I'll get a lift back from my cousin. Maybe we can all three go to dinner."

I was already considering having my dinner with a certain scientist, but I didn't bring it up. One mutiny at a time.

After depositing Harry, I used his car phone to call the college switchboard operator, who put me through to the psychology department. I learned that Professor Garrity had left for the day. Only an hour earlier, that news would have sent me scrambling for some way to obtain her home address. But I'd since seen inside her confidential Seetak folder. Garrity's address had been one of the few items of information in the report that I'd actually understood.

The address was in Brookline, a very nice area southeast of the college. The Lexus was right at home there, even if its driver wasn't. We cruised the tree-lined streets together until I spotted the right one, Heath Walk, and the right house, a dark green Queen Anne on a terraced lot. I parked across the street.

By then I was second-guessing the whole expedition. It had finally occurred to me that I'd be as likely to find Wayne Woodson at home as Garrity. And I didn't want to face the two of them together. I thought about circling the block to give me time to call the English department and get Woodson's class schedule. Before I could act on the impulse, I saw his wife coming down their front walk.

Garrity was wearing an old windbreaker and jeans, sneakers and work gloves. She carried an empty bushel basket and a pair of garden shears. She didn't look up as I exited the sedan or when it beeped to tell me that it had locked itself and I shouldn't worry. By then the professor had crouched beside the ground cover that bordered her walk. She lifted a long runner, froze for a beat, and then looked my way.

I'd received many an unwelcoming look over the years, but Garrity's raised the bar. "This is insupportable, Mr. Keane. You have no right to intrude here, whatever claims you may have to business with the college."

I was struck by the sharp-edged half moons of skin under her eyes and the deep lines that circled her neck. I realized that I'd been picturing her as she'd looked in the painting in Woodson's office. As young and happy.

"I'm not here about college business," I said.

"What do you want then?" As she asked, she glanced nervously toward the house. I decided that Garrity was as worried as I was over the possibility that Woodson might intrude.

"I've come to ask you about rape."

"I can recommend a book or two."

"I don't have time for that." She was turned toward the house again. "Maybe you could show me around your neighborhood while we talk."

Garrity looked up and down the sunlit Brookline street as though it were a trail through a jungle. Her earlier judgment that I was nonthreatening seemed to have been revised. "I don't think so."

"Fine. I'm comfortable standing here."

The professor was not. "Five minutes," she said. "That's all."

I noted that while she left her gloves and basket behind, she kept her shears. She walked us uphill, past other gardeners, trying to jump start the reluctant spring, and children, some still in school uniforms.

"What is it you want to know?" Garrity asked after we'd knocked off the first block.

"When we spoke to you on Monday, you mentioned

something you called anger rape. I'd like to hear more about that.''

Garrity seemed surprised by the question. I was a little surprised myself. ''Anger rape isn't my term,'' she said. ''It's a recognized category of rape.''

''But it's the one you're most interested in.''

''Who told you that?''

''You said the Cleveland Circle rape began your interest in the subject. That you'd begun by trying to understand that rape.''

''From which you infer that my area of special interest has remained anger rape. You're right, as it happens.''

''So tell me about it.''

''Where to begin? You know from the Cleveland Circle attack that anger rape is particularly brutal. Unlike other types of rape, it isn't about exerting control or exercising power. Not in a general sense. It's about releasing anger. Enormous, highly compressed anger. Anger the rapist himself may not be aware he's carrying.

''For that reason, these attacks are characterized by extensive physical trauma for the victim. By that I mean both severe trauma and widespread trauma. The rapist strikes his victim on every surface that comes to hand and does it with a ferocity, a rapidity that seems non-human, something more akin to cartoon violence than anything one human being could do to another.

''The unnatural intensity of the attack may contribute to a feeling of dissociation experienced by the rapists. Many of them have told me that they felt more like an onlooker than a participant in the attack.''

''You've spoken to these rapists?''

''Of course I have, Mr. Keane. You can't understand the psychology of rape by talking to the victims, many of whom are unwilling or unable to talk about it in any case. You have to go to the source. When I interview anger rapists, I consistently hear that the assailants didn't plan their attacks, that they often couldn't anticipate them. Anger rapists strike infrequently and choose their victims randomly. Or what seems to them to be randomly. It's all part of the impression they have that events are out of their control. That mindset may be another contributor to the phenomenon of dissociation.''

"Could the dissociation account for the fact that no semen was left by the Cleveland Circle rapist?''

"Possibly. That's certainly a more intelligent surmise than the police were able to produce in 1969. They believed that any rape was primarily a sexual act, a misconception as old as mankind. So they saw Francine Knaff's beating as the result of her assailant's inability to perform sexually. It's more likely that his sexual impulses were simply subsumed in the ferocity of the physical assault.''

Two power walkers approached us around a bend in the sidewalk. They were dressed in warm-up suits made of old circus tents and they were armed with tiny dumbbells. We ceded the concrete and waited for them to pass, Garrity looking up at the sky as we stood on the grass verge. It had started to cloud over again, but she was still able to judge the time.

"Your five minutes are about up,'' she said.

"Have you developed a profile for the anger rapist?''

"Profiling is somewhat overrated, as trendy ideas tend to be. Still, we can make some generalizations. The anger rapist tends to be a loner. Not from a lack of social skills necessarily, but from an inward inclination to avoid close relationships. In other words, he may have many acquaintances but no real friends. He'll also have an ambivalent attitude toward women: a tendency to elevate them and a deep-rooted suspicion that they're unworthy of elevation. Similarly, he'll have a confused attitude toward sex, possibly as a result of a strict upbringing or even childhood sexual abuse. Sex will be important to him, but he'll tend to consider the sex act to be dirty or debased.''

Garrity had been looking up at the clouds and her tone had been that of a seasoned lecturer. Now her voice lost its classroom quality.

''There's often a trigger incident. An upsetting event involving an important woman in the rapist's life. A female figure of authority. Or an object of sexual desire. In the ensuing attack, the victim is the accidental surrogate for this significant female figure, an innocent victim of the anger the rapist feels for another.''

Garrity looked down from the sky with an effort. ''Please don't come to my house again, Mr. Keane.''

TWENTY-ONE

GARRITY DIDN'T invite me to walk with her back down the hill. I waited for a few minutes where she'd left me, intending only to give her a head start before retrieving the Lexus. But when the few minutes had passed, I continued up the hill, in the direction we'd been headed when the power walkers surprised us.

After that I chose my route at random, as I had on the night of the Cleveland Circle attack. I was back in that night mentally, but not because my aimless walking had jogged a memory. Garrity's lecture had. Her closing remarks had. The part of the tragic evening I revisited was the period that had so interested my police interrogators: the unaccounted-for hour before my solo walk in the rain.

I'D SPENT that hour with Mary Fitzgerald in a room we'd borrowed from a friend of Mary's. The room was in one of the college's other Cleveland Circle acquisitions, the one directly behind Two Sutherland, a much larger building that had multiple two-and three-bedroom apartments on each floor. Mary and I had borrowed an entire apartment, Mary's friend's roommates having scattered for the weekend. That fit into our plans nicely, because what we were really trying to borrow wasn't an apartment or a room. It was a bed.

We hadn't had sex before, together or separately, though we'd been inching toward it since the holidays. In our inexperience, we overplanned this first real attempt, or so I rationalized things later. The secrecy. The sneaking around. Even the cheap wine, loud music, and soft lighting played on our nerves. On my nerves.

Mary didn't need to employ cosmetic lighting or to ply her lovers with vin rosé. She was simply and completely beautiful. The most beautiful thing I'd seen in my eighteen years. Her skin cool and white on that March night. Her slender body perfect. Unmarked. Untouched until I touched it.

Not that her more-than-imagined beauty worked in my favor. Quite the contrary. It was so overwhelming to me that our lovemaking ended before it had really begun. Certainly before it had begun for Mary. She was kind, but her solicitude and her unskilled attempts to coax me into a second try only added to my humiliation. And shame. I dressed and took the building's old cage elevator down to the first floor alone.

I stepped out onto Chestnut Hill Avenue and into a rain that seemed expressly made for a mood of extreme self-pity. Because of the rain there were few people about. But if a parade had been passing, I think I would still have spotted him. Harry, whose feelings for Mary had grown so obvious even I was aware of them. He was standing across the avenue, under the overhanging roof of the municipal skating rink, watching the building I had just left. Watching me leave it with a look of pure hatred on his face.

Despite all our secrecy and our elaborate evasions, Harry had known what Mary and I had been up to. I decided, irrationally, that he also knew how I'd performed, how I'd wasted all that Mary had tried to give me. I was about to turn and run when, unexpectedly, Harry did, slipping into the darkness of the mothballed rink.

In that instant, I switched from pursued to pursuer. I

dodged through the traffic on Chestnut Hill and vaulted the half wall of the empty rink. Harry had disappeared. I listened to the sound of the rain pounding the rink's picnic-shelter roof. Then I started walking.

I FOUND Garrity's gloomy house again without looking for it. Dusk had snuck up on me as I'd wandered. Lights were visible through the Queen Anne's first-floor windows. I watched those faint yellow lights for a time, waiting for a glimpse of Garrity or Woodson or a plan. None of the three appeared, so I got into the Lexus and left.

I was in no mood by then for dinner with Rebecca Wiese. Or anyone else. I thought about driving around until the two Harrys got tired of waiting for me, but I didn't do it. I told myself that before I could decide whether to go along with the official program, I had to know what that program was.

I left the car on the Dominion's crescent drive and crossed the lobby like a fugitive, afraid that Melanie Murray would tug at my sleeve any second. I made it to an elevator unaccosted and ascended to the suite, steeling myself for Harry's bulldozer questioning.

The bulldozer wasn't in. I looked everywhere, including his whirlpool bathtub. The only sign I found that anyone had been there since the maid was a bottle of Marker's Mark on the bar next to an empty rocks glass that had recently held bourbon, the single glass suggesting that Gilder had had a better dinner offer.

On my second circuit through the suite, I noticed that the message light on the little desktop computer was lit. I flipped it open and checked my pigeonhole, expecting an electronic reprimand from my roommate. My mailbox was empty. I checked Harry's next, hoping for another rambling audio message from Amanda. I found a brief typed message. "Wait for me on the reservoir trail. Important." It was signed Owen.

I crossed to the picture window. I could see a tiny figure on the northern bank of the reservoir, directly beneath one of the halogen lights. Harry.

The elevator I'd ridden up had gone. I called another and paced back and forth, banging the call button each time I passed it. Once inside a golden car and dropping, I held in the button for the lobby. The superstition paid off for me; the elevator made the entire trip without a stop.

Next I blundered around the lobby trying to find the exit for the jogging path. I could have looked for a security guard or a policeman while I was at it, but I didn't. At the bottom of the flight of stairs that led to the hotel's exercise room and pool, I found the exit and charged through it.

Once outside on the gravel path, I broke into a run. That was a mistake. I was years past having the wind to cover the distance at anything better than a brisk walk. I was struggling to breathe long before I neared Harry.

He saw me coming but didn't stir from the bright circle of pink light. He had no reason to stir, since I was exactly what he'd been expecting to see. I tried to call to him to get out of the light, but I couldn't generate the volume. He continued to stand on the edge of the rocky bank, puffing on his cigar and enjoying my struggles.

I was ten feet from him when the first shot rang out. Harry turned toward the sound, which had come from the wooded hillock behind him, missing my last desperate burst of speed and my flying tackle. I blindsided him, sending us both tumbling into the water.

TWENTY-TWO

I HEARD HARRY grunt as we hit the water. As he hit something that wasn't water. The second shot sounded an instant later, claiming the bulk of my attention. The shot and the water, so cold there should have been ice, claimed my attention, but I still heard Harry's grunt and filed it away. When we came to the surface and he just lay there, I knew he'd hit his head on something.

Just what was anybody's guess. As I rolled him onto his back and held his face clear of the water, I remembered a drought that had emptied the reservoir of Trenton, New Jersey, my hometown. They'd found shopping carts, bed frames, and even an example of that ubiquitous Jersey artifact, the oil drum, on the exposed bottom. There was no telling what the enterprising citizens of Chestnut Hill had deposited in their reservoir, fence or no fence.

My speculations on the subject were cut short by the third shot. I actually saw it strike the water just beyond us. I also heard or felt it through the water: an off-key pluck on a taut string.

I kicked us toward the protection of the sloping rock and concrete bank, knowing that if the gunman chose to come down from the concealment of the wooded hill, the bank would be no protection at all. I tried to rouse Harry, swallowed water as his weight pushed me under, and felt something solid underfoot. The edge of the bank. I struggled out of my topcoat one arm at a time, my splashing around drawing the fourth shot, which ricocheted off the stone just above us.

I started to edge us toward the hotel, pushing off on the slanted bottom, slipping as much as pushing, with both arms under Harry's. He was definitely settling as his cashmere coat soaked up the water, and I was already tired, my breathing still shallow from my run. But I made progress. The fifth bullet skipped across the black swells well behind us, near the watery grave of my new coat.

Through all of it I could hear the traffic on Chestnut Hill Avenue, the screech of brakes, horns solo and in angry pairs, the rhythmic thumping of stereos. I heard it and I thought, Why aren't they helping us? Can't they hear the gunshots? Are gunshots something they hear every day?

Frustrated, I pushed too hard against the slimy bottom and sent us into deep water again. We both went under, and I came up sputtering. Harry did, too, which I noted as I struggled, certain there'd be another shot now that I'd telegraphed our position. We were back in the shadow of the bank when it came. It sounded different from the others. Flatter. And I never heard the bullet strike water or stone.

That shot was the one I'd been waiting for, the sixth. After that there were only the sounds of traffic and the water slapping at the rocks.

Harry must have been counting, too, on some half-conscious level. "Revolver," he groaned. "Right again, God damn it."

"If you can bitch, you can kick. Give me some help here."

He didn't answer me or help. I struggled on, wondering how long it took to reload a revolver in the dark. Murray's killer hadn't reloaded, but then that job had been more than complete. Minutes passed and the firing didn't resume. I decided it wasn't going to.

By then I was more preoccupied with the cold and with Harry. My feet and hands were aching, and I'd begun to shake. Whether that was a reaction to the cold or the target practice, I couldn't say. Harry hadn't spoken again, which worried me more than his initial silence. I tried to get him out of his coat, but he seemed to have swollen inside it and I nearly drowned us trying.

During the rest break that followed the attempt, I considered the problem of climbing out of the water. The bank was a wall of breakwater-size stones, the smallest as large as a big-screen television. For their size they were smoothly finished, but there were still handholds in the stones themselves and between them. Not deep ones, but the slope of the bank was such that you could almost lie on it as you climbed. I could have made it without Harry. With him, it was all I could do to keep our heads above water.

I called to him, my chattering teeth making a meal of his name. "Wake up. I need you to hold on to the rocks while I go for help. Harry!"

I shook him, barely moving his sodden bulk, wondering if I'd waited too long, if I was too spent to make the climb. While I wondered, I clung to the top edge of the nearest rock with my left hand, my right arm around Harry. Above us, fragments of cloud, almost white with the reflected light of the city, tore across a black sky, its few faint stars only accentuating its emptiness.

But the sky wasn't empty. A jet, bound for Logan Airport, passed overhead, as stately as an ocean liner. I had an impulse to call out and almost laughed at myself. Instead I did call out, not to the plane but to the world in general.

"Help! Somebody help us!" I'd left that too long, too.

My voice barely carried, even with the lake as sounding board.

Then Harry raised his head and said, "Mary?" His tone was casual surprise, the tone you'd use to greet some acquaintance you hadn't expected to see. Not the correct way to address a wife dead nine years.

"Harry," I said. "Listen to me—"

"Mary!" Harry called out, so urgently now that I looked up myself. He'd met her once before since her funeral. On a lonely beach, he'd reached his hand out from the private hell where he'd kept himself since her death and felt her take it.

That's what he'd told me afterward. I'd witnessed the miracle, but at a distance. I'd seen Harry reach out his hand, but that was all I'd seen. All I'd believed.

I was close enough now to see better. If Harry reached out his hand again, I'd be ready. I'd grab whatever grabbed him and hold on.

Harry didn't reach out or call Mary's name again. His head lolled back against my shoulder. The shoulder that was ready to come apart. I released my hold and pushed off again. And again and again. We arrived at the next halogen light. By my rough calculation, we'd reach the Dominion just about the time the world-famous breakfast buffet opened.

"All you can eat," I said to the lamppost above us.

Harry said, "What?" And then expanded on the idea: "What the hell?"

I wondered how long he'd be with me this visit. And if together we might still climb out. The bank, thrown into sharp relief by the light, looked as easy to climb as a staircase. Just then, though, I wasn't sure I could handle an escalator.

Before I could work out a plan, I heard footsteps on

the gravel path. They were coming from the direction of the hotel. Two runners? Three.

I tried for another handhold but couldn't reach my arm high enough.

Harry was yelling now and moaning between yells. A figure appeared on the bank above us, silhouetted in the pink light. It held a gun with both hands.

"Two in the water, Inez," the figure, a policeman, said. "Cover me. I'm going down."

TWENTY-THREE

OUR RESCUERS were two uniformed cops and a hotel security guard, also uniformed, his getup fancy enough for the Joint Chiefs of Staff. Though overdressed, he was the best prepared of the three, since he'd thought to bring along a nylon rope with a white plastic buoy tied to one end. They used the rope to haul Harry out. I felt so light without him that I decided I didn't need any help, that I could climb out all by myself. When I'd worked through that delusion, they used the rope on me.

Once we were all together on the jogging path, the cops were faced with a dilemma: keep Harry still until an ambulance arrived or find some less exposed place to be. The cold decided the issue as much as the threat of another barrage. We made for the Dominion, the security guard and the first cop supporting Harry, me supporting myself, and Inez covering our backs.

We caused a little stir in the ground floor exercise room, scaring the business-class clientele off their stair machines and treadmills. Harry was the principal cause. That is, the freely bleeding gash on his forehead was. I forced myself to examine his wound and came away encouraged. It didn't look much worse than the bloody but superficial cut I'd recently collected in a car wreck.

While the police tended to Harry, I had a moment to talk to the security guard, to thank him and ask him how they'd noticed us finally. In my chattering, exhausted state, I was hoping he'd say that a beautiful woman with honey-colored hair had appeared out of nowhere and tipped him off, perhaps pointing a long white arm at the reservoir without speaking.

The guard said, "How'd we notice you? You kidding? We heard the shots. Sounded like a fucking turkey shoot."

"Then what took you so long?"

"What long? We waited for the cops to get here. Maybe five minutes."

I'd have said twenty-five, had I been asked. But when the police got around to asking me questions, that one didn't come up. Harry, though conscious, was groggy, especially on the subject of how he'd come to be in the reservoir. So the cops put it to me next.

I drew my borrowed towel tighter around my shoulders. "My friend was smoking a cigar. I was going out to meet him. Someone started shooting at us from the hillside. I don't know who. I couldn't see anything. The only place we could go was in the water." I added, "We're from out of town," hoping that would make my half answers sound more plausible.

It didn't seem to have that effect, so I worked another angle. "My friend's cousin is on your force. Lieutenant Harry Gilder. He'll want to know what's happened."

That and the arrival of the ambulance got me off the hook. I rode with Harry to St. Elizabeth's Medical Center, listening to him tell me over and over that he didn't want me calling Amanda and worrying her.

When I'd finally convinced him I wouldn't call her, Harry asked, "How did anyone know we'd be out there? Were you with someone when you left me that message?"

"I didn't leave you any message. It was a phony."

Harry thought about it with his eyes closed. He looked

like he was hiding behind the fat dressing on his head. "You knew it was a trap," he murmured. "How?"

"I saw the message to you. I knew I hadn't left it."

Harry's eyes opened. "I deleted the message."

Once at the hospital, a huge complex just off Chestnut Hill Avenue at Cambridge Street, we were separated. I was given a place to towel off—though by then I was only damp—and a cursory examination. I was still seated on the examination table, considering whether to trade my thin but dry hospital gown for my ruined suit, when Gilder came in.

For once he resembled his cousin. It was because he was angry at me, as Harry so often seemed to be. "I hope you're happy," he said. "They're sewing Harry's scalp up now. He's here for tonight at least. For observation."

Gilder was right up against me, his red face in mine. I drew my knees together, forcing him back a step. "So he's okay?"

"His skull's not fractured, no thanks to you."

He hadn't been shot either, which was thanks to me. But Gilder didn't let me pat my naked back.

"Harry told me this afternoon how little help you've been on this, how you've been spaced out since the two of you came up here. Daydreaming while he's been working. I saw it for myself that morning in my office. You were only half there and maybe not half. Harry's had to take the lead in everything. That's why he was the target tonight. Whoever did the shooting figured Harry was the reason you two came to Boston. But I'm thinking you're the reason. I think you're responsible for the mess Harry got into in 1969."

I was in danger of drifting off to daydream land again. Instead of listening to Gilder's tirade, I was wondering why it was bothering me so little. One possibility was a residual peace of mind, an afterglow from having gotten out of the reservoir alive. Another was that a cop leaning into me, his spittle hitting my face, was more comfortable for me than Gilder's earlier bonhomie. It was what I was used to.

"Harry wasn't the target tonight," I said. "Not Harry alone. Whoever set that up wanted both of us. Harry was smoking away in full view for the better part of a long cigar. The gunman could have shot him a dozen times. He didn't try until I got there."

"Coincidence," Gilder snapped. "The shooter wasn't ready to fire until you showed up. He couldn't know where Harry was going to decide to stand and smoke his cigar. It took him a while to place himself after Harry came to rest."

There was something in that. No one could have known what spot on the reservoir path Harry would instinctively choose for our rendezvous. No one but me.

"And the phony message on the suite's computer," Gilder was saying. "It was for Harry, not you."

"It was for both of us. Didn't Harry tell you he deleted the message after he'd read it?"

"He's still confused," Gilder said.

"Not about that. He deleted the message and someone put it back. We were both lured out there by the same bait, Harry because he didn't know it was a trap and me because I did."

Gilder backed up a step. I must have passed out of visual range, because he started to squint. "How do you leave those messages?"

"From terminals in any of the hotel rooms or in the lobby. The system may keep a log of where messages are entered."

"I'll check on that," he said, still angry but less so. He was willing to concede now that my life had been in as much danger as Harry's. But his other charge—that I was responsible for Harry's involvement in the case— still hung in the antiseptic air. Gilder was welcome to blame me for that, I decided.

The door creaked behind him and a nurse stuck her head in. She looked at me over her reading glasses, critically. "Still here, Mr. Keane? You weren't admitted, you know. You have to find another place to sleep tonight. We need this room."

I might have come back with a snappy answer if a large percentage of me hadn't been exposed to the hallway draft. "On my way," I said.

Gilder stayed to watch me dress. He took my seat on the end of the examination table, causing a jolt of déjà vu that I couldn't explain away until I remembered Detective Craney, watching my haircut from a table perch, circa 1969.

Gilder was still cooling down, or pretending to. "Sorry I pulled my Joe Pesci on you just now. That call about Harry scared me to death. I'm supposed to be looking after the guy. I could have kissed all future Thanksgiving dinners good-bye if this had been serious. That's the way the family feels about Harry. I'll be in enough trouble if this makes the paper. I'll try to see it doesn't."

"I should check on Harry," I said.

"We'll look after him tonight," Gilder said, his nose hardening again, if only briefly. "What about you? You feel safe going back to the hotel?"

I shrugged, summing the matter up for both of us.

The lieutenant offered to drive me back to the Dominion. I accepted, figuring I'd be closer to the heater in his car than in a taxi—I was—and that his ulterior motive was a crack at the hotel staff—it wasn't. Gilder wasn't finished with me yet. As soon as we were safely belted in, he dug out the eyeglasses whose existence I'd deduced back in his office. They made him look more dangerous. Craftier. When we were rolling, he moved on to the big question, the one I'd started working over as soon as I knew Harry was okay. Namely, what did the ambush tell us about the world we lived in?

"Harry filled me in this afternoon on the DNA test that Garrity woman commissioned."

Harry in his short-lived moment of triumph. "Did he?"

"We'll call it a tip from an anonymous source when we visit Seetak tomorrow."

"'We?' I didn't think you were assigned to this case."

"I can wrangle an invite. I think I'd better after tonight."

Thanksgiving insurance, I thought.

"The thing is," Gilder continued, "Harry never got around to explaining the connection between Garrity and Murray. He acted coy about it—he'd had a drink or two—but I wasn't sure he really knew."

"He doesn't."

"Do you?"

We stopped for a traffic signal. On the corner nearest my side of the car, four young men were smoking and jockeying for the center of a circle of light cast by a street lamp. Two of the four took the competition more seriously than the others, and a shoving match broke out. Gilder glanced over, noted that the two youths were smiling and laughing, and turned back to the traffic light.

"So do you?" he asked again when the light turned green.

"I've got an idea," I said. "A hunch."

"Let's hear it."

"I'd like to work on it a little first."

"Listen, Keane. Tell me what your idea is, and I'll work on it. It's not safe for you to be an independent operator anymore. What happened tonight says that if it says anything."

What the events of the evening said to me was "You can't afford another misstep."

"I can't tell you," I said. "Not yet." Gilder took his foot off the accelerator. "It's Harry's call. He's in charge of this. You said so yourself. I owe it to him to run my idea past him first. If he thinks there's anything to it, he'll tell you."

It was the part I'd played for Koie Mustafa: Harry's loyal assistant. It had satisfied her, and it satisfied Gilder. He hit the gas again, hard.

"Talk to Harry first thing in the morning," he said.

TWENTY-FOUR

I WAS TOO WEARY to play Gilder's shadow as he poked around the Dominion, even if he'd been in the mood for a shadow. Too weary and too conspicuous in my drip-dry attire. But I was lonely, too, an odd reaction for a man who passed most of his evenings hugging a book. I'd gotten used to having Harry's company again faster than I would have guessed possible. I said good night to his cousin reluctantly. And when I passed Melanie Murray's usual easy chair and found it empty, I was almost disappointed. Almost.

Once inside the suite with the dead bolt thrown and the security chain in place, all closets opened and both beds looked under, I took a long hot shower. Then I put on one of the Dominion's fleecy robes and visited the suite's bar. I'd resisted the temptation to have a scotch the day before in the Last Stand. Now I poured myself a double. My first hard liquor of 1995. If I'd learned nothing else in my sixteen years of Catholic school, it was that life was stumbling and rising again.

I took my drink to the picture window and its view of the reservoir. The investigation of the attempted shooting was either finished or on hold until sunup; no one was about.

I fell into thinking about the spot where Harry had chosen to wait for me, which led me back to our college days again, my backward slide greased by the scotch. This time my destination was the spring of 1972, the last semester of my last year at Boston College. Of our last year, Mary's and Harry's and mine.

I'D MADE IT to the eve of graduation in spite of my ongoing fascination with mysteries. My compulsive questioning had resulted in a spotted academic career, and my unofficial career—amateur meddler in police business—had been just as uneven. I'd had my successes, but they'd been offset by one high-profile failure, which had resulted in my arrest on the center of campus as most of the student body, gathered for a late antiwar rally, had looked on. The charge had been drug dealing, and I'd cleared myself easily. But I'd never learned the identity of the real pusher, who had, I believed, deliberately poisoned a friend of Mary's.

On the profit side of the ledger was the arrest and conviction of my old nemesis, the Oldsmobile Bandit. He'd continued to prey on coed hitchhikers and I'd kept after him, though I'd changed my tactics to keep peace with Harry. I'd seized on the color of the bandit's car, the only solid clue any of the victims had been able to provide. I'd checked a hunch and found that Oldsmobile hadn't offered a metallic green paint until well after the likely model year of the coupe in question. I'd then begun to telephone or visit every paint shop in the Boston area, a hobby that had taken up most of my sophomore year. Harry had derided the search, saying, reasonably enough, that if the bandit happened to be from out of town, I'd spend the rest of my life tracing him. Mary had encouraged me, perhaps as a way of keeping me out of more serious trouble. In the end, I'd surprised all of us by identifying a suspect and, with Harry's help, catching him in the act.

On the afternoon I'd drifted back to, a Saturday afternoon in May 1972, I'd been waiting for Mary on the asphalt plaza in front of McElroy, where she and I had waited together for the Cleveland Circle shuttle bus as freshmen. On this particular Saturday we were meeting either to study for finals or to have sex. It said a lot about the state of our relationship that I wasn't sure which we'd do, wasn't sure which Mary would want to do. I was changing my mind about which I wanted with every pass across the tarmac.

Our relationship if graphed would have been a parabola, the classic shape for a college romance. We'd grown closer and closer, sexually more and more intimate, and then we'd begun to slowly draw apart. The peak had been very near the halfway point of our college careers, the point of no return, the moment when there had been as much college behind us as ahead of us and every day that passed had been a reminder that the real world was waiting to pounce. Mary and I never discussed the time after BC—never seriously discussed it—and that conscious and unconscious omission had subtly pulled us apart.

The day was warm, almost too warm for the exposed plaza, though it was early enough in the year for the heat to be a welcome novelty. I was thinking of Cleveland Circle, either because of my proximity to our old bus stop or because it was natural to be thinking back on the first time Mary and I had made love on the eve of what might be the last time.

The heat finally drove me to McElroy's covered entrance. I paced in the shade of the flat aluminum awning, getting in the way of people entering and leaving the building. I was thinking of Francine Knaff by then and not looking where I was going. As a result, I was nearly knocked down when one of the big aluminum and glass doors was slammed open by a speeding coed. I caught the door defensively and held it open. Taped to the glass, an inch from my nose, was a poster advertising Gay Pride Day, an event sponsored by the Greater Boston Homophile League. It was taking place that very afternoon on the Boston Common.

I looked around, wondering how I'd leave a message for Mary, and spotted her crossing College Road on her way to our rendezvous, her old green jacket worn like a cape across her shoulders. I ran to her, babbled an explanation, and took off down College to the parking space where I'd left my car. My new old car, a 1965 Volkswagen Karmann-Ghia.

Though I was in a hurry, I made a quick pass around the little coupe to make sure no one had initialed its red paint. I spotted only those defects I already knew about, the bubbled paint on the rocker panels and around the protruding fifties headlights. The bubbles were warning signs of imminent rust-through, but I'd convinced myself that they were only temporary swellings caused by the heat.

The inside of the car was hot enough to support the diagnosis. I popped the rear vent windows, lowered the front ones with the sole surviving window crank, which I kept in the glove compartment for safekeeping. Before starting the engine, I rattled the gearshift lever, a little therapy I'd worked out to cure my habit of starting the car in gear. Then I was off in a cloud of blue smoke: down College to Commonwealth and Commonwealth to the city.

TWENTY-FIVE

TRAFFIC WAS LIGHT, it being Saturday, but parking was scarce downtown, especially around the Common. I'd underestimated the crowd that Gay Pride Day would draw, picturing something on the order of Boston College's annual activities fair—the event where Murray had discovered Shakespeare—a few underengineered booths which the campus rank and file gave a wide berth. Instead I found that the Common east of Frog Pond had been almost completely taken over by the rally.

The sight of the teeming hillside almost made me give up my search before I started. The object of it was a single gay man who had been a freshman at BC in 1968 and a short-time resident of Two Sutherland Road: Steven Stapella. Stapella had run afoul of Tregnab and other enlightened members of the dorm for hanging a Boston Homophile League poster. When I'd seen the poster on McElroy's door, I'd thought of Stapella for perhaps the first time since he'd dropped out. And I'd known I had to find him.

The proposition had seemed straightforward enough on the student union plaza. If Stapella was still in the Boston area, he might still be a member of the Homophile League. So I only had to find the people in charge and ask. Easy. Except that no one seemed to be in charge, not even at the epicenter of the rally, a platform on a rise near Park Street, where different speakers jostled for control of the microphone, while independents, with and without bullhorns, shouted them down.

Different groups had set up tables or booths or had simply gathered beneath banners tied to trees. I picked a group at random, asked for Stapella, got a no, and went on to the next. Through this process, I accidentally found the Homophile League's home base, a table set up in a shady grove far from the excitement of the speaker's platform. The lone man staffing the table had only recently opted for the shade. He was shirtless, sleepy-eyed, and badly sunburned.

In response to my standard question, he repeated Stapella's name so often it began to sound unlikely to me, a name I'd dreamed or imagined.

"The thing is, we've got hundreds of members. So one name doesn't mean too much. It is familiar, though. What you have to do is come by our office on Monday. But not too early on Monday. Wait. Take some literature. I'm stuck here until I get rid of it."

I gathered up some leaflets and was turning away when the sunburned man said, "Try the Roxbury chapter. They're set up by Frog Pond. We asked the groups to identify themselves by area so people would know we're everywhere. Roxbury and Stapella sound right together for some reason."

I followed up the tip, but slowly, stopping to ask my question of every friendly face. The Roxbury contingent was the last stop before the artificial pond. They were seated on its concrete bank, four men, two of whom were cooling their feet in the shallow water. When they offered me a beer, I sat down, too, though I kept my Adidas dry. The four had never heard of Stapella. Like just about everyone else I'd asked, they misinterpreted my interest in him, inviting me to forget him and join them at a party in Cambridge.

I was ready to take the first part of their advice and

give up. The rally was ending, or at least moving on. I finished my beer, thanked the Roxbury four, and started for the side street where I'd left the Ghia.

I hadn't gone far before a hand-lettered sign taped to a lamppost caught my eye. The cardboard sheet was curling in on itself, but I could just make out the name West Roxbury. Two men were bracing the lamppost between them. One of them was Steven Stapella.

"Owen Keane," he said as I walked up. "I always knew I'd see you at one of these sooner or later."

"Did you?" I said. "I'm surprised you remember me."

"And vice versa. You didn't have two words for me in the old days. Not that I recall. Intense and brooding. Those are two words for you. That's how I thought of Owen Keane."

Pale and thin was how I remembered Stapella. He was still rail thin, but he was now so tanned that I suspected a sun lamp. Tanned with a single earring and thin straight hair worn at shoulder length, a little longer than my own. His face reminded me, as it always had, of the television cowboy Roy Rogers, every feature thin, even his eyes. He wore an almost sleeveless striped T-shirt and jeans.

"Does your mother know you're smoking?" he asked, his hand out, first to point to the pack in my shirt pocket, then to accept the cigarette I shook from it. I took one, too, and lit them both.

"Owen Keane. I remember I was shocked when I heard you were one of the guys who spoke up for me."

"What happened with that?"

"I don't want to talk about it. Not on a beautiful positive-energy day like today. Anyway, you don't talk about bad things at a reunion. Only the good stuff. If there wasn't any good stuff, you make some up. With Boston College and me, it's more made up than not.''

"Where did you go? I mean, what school?''

"No school right away. No, wait. I should have said the school of hard knocks. That would have been better. I went out to the West Coast. You wouldn't believe how crazy it is out there. Too crazy for me. And too straight. At least where I ended up. I guess you could say I fell in with the wrong crowd. So I came back.''

"When?''

"All this interest in me. So much easier to chitchat than to talk about the really important things, isn't it?''

"This is important, Steven.''

"Really? Then let's see. I was away a year. I came back right after the holidays. January 1970. Start of a clean decade, now hopelessly sullied.''

"When you got back did you hear about an attack near Cleveland Circle?''

"An attack? No.'' Stapella smiled as though he was considering making a joke. Then he repeated, ''No.''

"A woman was raped and beaten to death.''

"Shit, Owen, that's terrible. I bet it shook up the little world of Two Sutherland.''

"It did,'' I said.

"No, I never heard about that. So much shit happening all the time these days. The war and everything. Even the horrors barely cause a ripple. Now let me ask you about Owen Keane. Or are you out of questions?''

"Just a couple more.'' One more actually, the one I'd come to ask. ''When you left BC, what did you do with your keys?''

"My keys?''

"Your room key and the one to the dorm's front

door." I attempted to lead my witness then, afraid of what he might tell me. "Did you give them to Foley?"

"That mick bastard? A lot of help he was when I needed him."

"Did you leave them with your roommate?"

"Wait a minute, let me think. No, I didn't leave them with Ellison. He was stoned as usual. Whatever happened to him, anyway?"

"Who got your keys?"

"Mellow out, Owen. I gave them to Alan Avery. The night I decided to leave—I said I wasn't going to tell you what they did to me and I won't—but that night I stopped by Alan's room. To thank him. I gave him my keys to turn in for me. I asked him to hold them for a while in case I changed my mind. Then turn them in.

"Are you okay, Owen? What's the big deal about the keys? Did they stick you for the deposit? Are you feeling sick?" He reached over and took my cigarette. "You're white. Is that beer I smell? How many have you had? You should know better than to drink and smoke in this sun."

"I'm okay," I said. "You're sure it was Avery?"

"Yes. Like I said, I wanted to thank him for trying to help and to say good-bye. I don't know, I might have been hoping he'd talk me out of leaving. He didn't try. He said he was sure I'd thought it all out. I hadn't, but hearing Alan say that made me feel as though I had.

"Poor Alan. He had a real gift with people. I hate like hell that he'll never get to use that gift."

"Because he didn't become a priest?" I asked, confused.

"A priest? Alan? Are you kidding?"

"What did you mean?"

Stapella now addressed me as though I'd been swimming in beer. "I meant since he's dead he'll never get to use his gift. You know, death, the great spoiler of potential. Wait a minute. You didn't know? I thought everybody would know."

"How did it happen?"

"He was killed in action. In 'Nam. I don't know how. Don't tell me you didn't know he was in Vietnam. You could have knocked me down with Nixon's fashion sense when I heard about it. Alan Avery in the marines. I don't think it tops the idea of Avery as a priest, though. Are you sure about that?"

"No," I said. I couldn't be sure about anything Avery had told me. "How did you hear this?"

"I wrote him from California. A long soul-baring letter. Alan had given me his home address the night I snuck out. He made me promise to write. His folks must have forwarded my letter because his reply came from a marine base where he was training. He was very supportive. He told me to be true to what I was. He said that was my only hope."

"What did he say about his own decision?"

"He didn't explain it, if that's what you mean. It wouldn't have been like Alan to explain. He just said it was something he had to do, like my going out to California. Only I came back.

"When I was back here and settled again, I called his mother to get an updated address. She told me Alan had tripped some kind of booby-trap. He'd been killed instantly."

I WANDERED AWAY from Stapella and the rally, ending up in Harry's old haunt, the combat zone. By 1972 I was old enough to drink legally anywhere, but I felt drawn that evening to places I had no business being. If I was looking for a knock on the head, I didn't get one. No one paid much attention to me. I drank until my money ran out. Then, though I shouldn't have, I drove myself back.

I ended up at the Chestnut Hill reservoir, at the end nearest Cleveland Circle. I sat down on the edge of the gravel path and cried.

Harry found me there sometime later. In my sodden state, that seemed almost miraculous.

"How?" I asked from my seat on the bank.

"Mary asked me to look for you. She got worried when you didn't come back. Actually, she's been worried since you left. Something you said to her about Cleveland Circle. I was on my way down there when I spotted your car. It's sticking halfway out into traffic, by the way."

There was only moonlight to work with, but Harry finally noticed that something was wrong. He sat down next to me. "What's happened?"

"Alan Avery was the Cleveland Circle rapist." I told him about Stapella's key, the key that had saved Avery when he'd lost his own at the scene of his crime.

Harry, being Harry, was skeptical. "So he had a replacement key. That doesn't prove he did it. I remember you saying that Avery was the only one who encouraged you to find the killer."

"He wanted to be found out and punished. He wanted me to be the one who did it. I let him down. So he took on the job himself."

I told Harry about Avery's enlistment and his end. The story got a low whistle out of Harry and something more. Grudging belief.

"He passed a death sentence on himself," Harry said. "Damn. And you solved it, Owen. It may have been too late from Avery's point of view, but you solved it. Damn.''

He stood up and pulled me after him. "Come on. Mary's sitting by the phone. Let's go back.''

TWENTY-SIX

I AWOKE the next morning on the Dominion's vast bed with no ill effects from my reservoir swim or my nightcaps plural. Of the two, I'd feared the scotch more, expecting the familiar ache between and behind my eyes and the old systemic aversion to the vertical. I experienced neither. What I did feel was something rare for me: an urgent desire to get on with the day.

I called St. Elizabeth's Medical Center, but not to talk to Harry. I was afraid to talk to him, even over the phone, afraid the promise I'd made to Gilder would kick in and I'd be demoted to the kind of role Murray the actor had specialized in. Spear carrier sans lines. The nurse who answered the phone on Harry's floor told me what I wanted to hear. He'd passed a peaceful night but wouldn't be discharged until ten at the earliest.

At eight-thirty I was on the already busy Boston College campus, climbing the stairs to the top floor of Carney Hall. I knew that at nine James Corbett would be lecturing on the novels of Ross Macdonald, and I wanted to talk with him first. He was in his time-share office, making his tin desk look like playroom furniture as he chuckled over a well-thumbed paperback. His delight in Macdonald's prose did a quick fade when he looked up and saw me in his doorway. I watched as he drank in the old trench coat I'd rescued from the trunk of the Lexus. Drank it in and gagged.

"Owen," he finally said. "I didn't expect to see you again this visit."

"You left so quickly the other day, I didn't get a chance to say good-bye. I'm heading back to New Jersey soon."

The promise relaxed Corbett visibly. "Come in, sit down. I've a few minutes before my class. Was your visit to Boston worthwhile? My wife said you told her you were up here on business. Sorry I didn't think to ask you myself."

"So far the trip's been okay," I said. "I won't really know for a while how things will pan out."

That vague answer more than satisfied what curiosity Corbett had. "Sounds like teaching," he said. "We can never guess how it will turn out, what use a student will make of what we've passed on. We seldom even hear about it." He made it sound as though not hearing was fine with him. It certainly beat having a promising student show up twenty-odd years down the road dressed in outerwear that featured a different style of button for every day of the week. "How did you get on with Wayne?"

"Fine," I said, disappointing Corbett, who must have been hoping for a little hair-pulling at least. "He has some intriguing ideas. Speaking of Woodson, I bumped into an alumnus yesterday who remembered him."

"An English major?" Corbett asked. "Who?"

I reached for a handy name. "Steven Stapella. He had Woodson for a course in the fall of 1968. He didn't remember much about the class, but he got fairly close to Woodson. Close enough for Woodson to confide in him. He told Stapella that he and his wife were anxious to have a child but that things weren't going well. I guess Woodson offered it up as an excuse. He was so distracted by the whole business his teaching had suffered."

Corbett leaned back in his chair and smiled. "I'd forgotten all about that."

I smiled, too. Harry had a well-connected gossip hound in Koie Mustafa, but I had a better one in James Corbett.

"I told you I'd mentored Wayne in his early days, didn't I?"

"Did you?" I asked innocently.

"Now that you mention the baby problems, it all comes back to me. How refreshing that was. Everybody else putting off families back then and these two young professionals so anxious to start one. The idea of it humanized Wayne so much, him wanting to be a father. He wasn't nearly the demigod then he's since become, but he had a certain confidence in his own opinions that could put me off. Then he'd unburden himself about the trouble he and Phyllis were having getting knocked up, and I'd actually start to like the guy."

"What was their problem?"

"Who knows? Wayne wasn't that forthcoming. He might not even have known exactly. I'm sure they didn't have all the tests back then we have today. They didn't have the treatment alternatives, either, the fertility drugs and the operations. The Woodsons were restricted to trying different sexual positions and keeping elaborate ovulation charts.

"Grace, our secretary, was telling me the other day about a friend of hers who had had an egg removed and fertilized with her husband's sperm in a laboratory, following which it was put back in—I shudder to think how. Quite an ordeal, but I'm sure Phyllis and Wayne would have gone through it in the old days if the procedure had been available."

So was I.

"Odd that I didn't think of Wayne when Grace was telling me that story. I was standing a few feet from his office door, too. Another reminder of how old I'm getting. Luckily, I forget those reminders fairly quickly. It worked, by the way.''

''What did?'' I asked, feeling older momentarily myself.

''The petri dish fertilization. Grace's friend had a healthy baby boy.''

We were running onto the berm. ''Whatever the Woodsons did worked, too,'' I said to draw us back.

''Yes. They had Bergen, Wayne's pride and joy.''

''But no brothers or sisters.''

''No. Nothing like the brood Jean and I raised.'' Corbett began to describe his own large family in such detail that I was certain the subject would carry us straight through to class time. Then he began to catalog his oldest son's football injuries, giving me the bridge I needed.

''That reminds me. My friend Stapella told me that he heard somewhere about Woodson's daughter being seriously ill. He said she needed a transfusion or maybe even a transplant. He wasn't exactly sure.''

''Bergen? When was this?''

''Fairly recently. In the last year or two.''

''I've never heard anything like that,'' Corbett said. ''I'm sure I would have, whatever my relationship with Wayne has become. No. I'm sure your friend was misinformed there. I've never heard anything but positives about Bergen. She's one lucky kid.''

I'D PARKED the Lexus illegally in a surface lot on lower campus. I began my walk to the car thinking about the hunch Corbett had confirmed and the one he'd failed to confirm. But before too long, I'd shifted my focus to Wayne Woodson and the fragmented lecture he'd given me on literary deconstruction.

At its most basic, deconstruction was a new way of

looking at an old story. Of finding new meanings in old texts, Rebecca Wiese had put it, but I wasn't that optimistic. The most I was hoping for was a new slant on the story Melanie Murray had been after, the one I'd been telling myself in bits and pieces ever since Harry had picked me up in New Brunswick. The Cleveland Circle mystery.

When I'd dropped in on Woodson, he'd been reading an essay about absence. The essay had been haunting me ever since, or its basic idea had, that the gaps or blanks in a story might be the key to understanding it. There were blanks in my story, most notably James Murray's absences from the Shakespeare rehearsals. More subtle was a related absence: the sudden disappearance of the torch Murray had been carrying for the troupe's blond Ophelia. Together the two absences suggested that Murray had shifted his attention to someone else, a woman he'd begun slipping out of the rehearsals to meet in the fall of 1968.

I'd glimpsed that much in 1969, when I'd first heard about Murray's disappearing act. But I'd never worked out his motivation. Why go to such elaborate lengths to meet a woman in secret during that breakthrough time when many couples were sleeping together openly, if not actually living together? Sally, the theater worker who had exploded Murray's alibi, had speculated that Murray had been meeting another guy's girlfriend. She'd been pointing me toward the truth, but I'd been distracted by thoughts of Murray the rapist, whom I'd pictured slipping away to stalk victims for months before he'd actually struck.

I'd walked past the Lexus somehow without spotting it. I would have been more likely to stop by a sixty-five Karmann-Ghia, given the temporal shifts I'd been experiencing. I was down by the new residence halls Harry had proudly pointed to on our first walk through the campus. One of the buildings held a cafeteria, if my nose was any guide. It led me to a double door, which a helpful student, looking not much older than Amanda Ohlman, held open for me.

On the other side I found a dining hall, as plush as a restaurant. That was plusher than it needed to be for me, since all I wanted was coffee. I filled a large Styrofoam cup at a self-service station and took it to the cash register before asking anyone if amateur detectives and other transients were served there. The cashier wasn't happy with me, but I had my money out and it was too late to pour the coffee back, so she rang me up.

Not wanting to overstay my welcome, I took the coffee outside, to a group of cement tables that were occupied only by a small flock of starlings on what had become another cool gray morning. I sat down and considered an absence I hadn't known about in 1969. The absence of a baby from Phyllis Garrity's womb. I'd told Corbett that Stapella had tipped me to that, but it had really been a guess prompted by my observation that the portrait of Bergen Woodson I'd seen in Woodson's office resembled Melanie Murray and Harry's follow-up remark about Wayne Woodson looking a little like James Murray. The guess, stimulated perhaps by Rebecca Wiese's long discourse on DNA and chromosomes and princes and princesses who lived happily ever after, had come to me sometime between my bath in the reservoir and my drive back to the Dominion with Harry Gilder. I'd gone to Corbett to confirm it, and he'd come through for me.

Phyllis Garrity had been unable to achieve a pregnancy with her husband. Lacking a medical miracle in that dark age, she'd come up with her own solution. She'd seduced a student, one who'd physically resembled Woodson. James Courtney Murray.

TWENTY-SEVEN

I WAS LATE getting to the hospital, which meant that Harry was late leaving it, since I had his shaving kit and a change of clothes. Fortunately for me, there'd been a paperwork snafu, so he would have been stuck there anyway. I found him in his private room, sitting on the edge of the tightly made bed, watching a daytime talk show whose subject—to judge by the looks of the panelists—could have been anything from "nose ring hygiene" to "tattoos as underwear."

Harry looked better than I'd expected, although unshaven and unnatty in his rented bathrobe. The dressing on his head, well above his left eyebrow, was a discreet adhesive patch, not the gauze turban I'd been imagining.

As I inspected him, he inspected me. "What happened to your new coat, Owen?"

"They're dragging the reservoir for it as we speak. Nice room."

It was, too. The floor was carpeted, and the walls were covered in two colors of vinyl wallpaper, cream over plum, the dividing line a heavy plastic chair rail.

"Never mind the room," Harry said. I'd made the mistake of mentioning the reservoir. Now we were stuck with the subject. "I've been thinking—in the clear moments between doses of pain killer—about what happened last night. You saved my life."

Again, his weary tone said. By my calculation he was still ahead on points in that particular competition.

"Tell that to your cousin," I said. "He thinks I bashed your head intentionally."

Harry looked as though he'd been considering that possibility himself, perhaps during his doses of painkiller. But he didn't say anything. He took the shaving kit and disappeared for fifteen minutes.

He emerged from the bathroom still thinking about my culpability. As he dressed in the striped shirt, navy slacks, and camel blazer I'd picked out for him, he asked, "What did you do yesterday after you dropped me downtown?"

I told him about my visit to Phyllis Garrity's dark Queen Anne.

"My cousin might have been right to chew you out," Harry said. "That little side trip might be what got us shot at."

"The timing would have been tight," I said.

"Too tight?"

"No." Thanks to my long pointless walk around Brookline, there would have been time.

"So tell me about this morning, Owen. I don't suppose you slept in."

I was watching the television. The topic of the show was neither nose rings nor tattoos. It was sexual obsessions between pets and owners.

Harry switched off the set. "Owen?"

"I couldn't sleep in. I promised your cousin I'd tell you about a hunch I had. I wanted to check it out first." I described my interview with Corbett and my surmise that Bergen Garrity-Woodson rated one more hyphen in her last name.

Harry sat down again on the bed. "Damn," he said. "Murray slept with Garrity back in sixty-eight?"

"And into sixty-nine. Right up until the time of the Cleveland Circle attack, if I'm guessing right. She se-

duced him, got pregnant by him, and dumped him. Somehow Woodson must have found out about it recently. I
don't know how. I asked Corbett if Bergen had had a
serious illness in the last year or so, something that would
have required a transfusion.''

"Or a transplant?" Harry asked. His dumbfounded
look had been replaced by a knowing smile. "Something
that would have required a donation from Woodson, only
the medical tests revealed that he wasn't capable of do-
nating, and—oh, by the way—couldn't possibly be Bergen's father?''

"What's so funny about that?"

"Nothing, except that it's a plot twist right out of those
paperbacks you love. A case of live by the sword, die by
the sword, I guess.''

"Can you think of another way Woodson could have
stumbled across the truth?''

"Yes," Harry said, still smiling, now with confidence.
"Murray could have told him. We know from Rita Murray that his relationship with Melanie had fallen apart
over the course of the last few years. Murray was a sentimental guy, doubly so when he'd been drinking. Suppose he started thinking about his firstborn, Bergen. Suppose he kept tabs on her through his college contacts.
Maybe though our old friend Koie Mustafa. He could
have gone from thinking about Bergen to wanting to meet
her, wanting to use her as a replacement in his life for
screwed-up Melanie. But he was an honorable guy, too.
So he approached Woodson alone or Garrity and Woodson together, exposing Garrity's secret.''

"You're assuming a fact not in evidence, counselor."

"Look who's talking," Harry smirked. But then,
"Namely?''

"That Murray knew he'd gotten Garrity pregnant in 1969."

Harry was cautiously exploring his dressing with his fingertips. He must have decided that a little more brain-work wouldn't cause a blowout because he said, "She had to get rid of him someway or other in sixty-nine. Why not by telling him the truth? How many college freshmen would hang around to embrace fatherhood if someone's holding the back door open for them?"

Harry took my silence for agreement and charged on.

"You're thinking that Woodson already knew a little about Murray from his wife's research on the Cleveland Circle rapist, right? She's been worried for twenty years that the student she picked to father her child might have gone on to be this terrible sexual predator. Hence her obsession with the case, which Woodson has absorbed like secondhand cigarette smoke. Then suddenly one of the prime suspects shows up and announces he's Bergen's father. So Woodson kills him."

"Wait up," I said. I'd brought Harry what I still considered to be a house of cards—that Murray was Bergen's father—and he was adding a game room and a sauna. "Now you're the one getting way ahead of what we know to be true."

"We know we were shot at last night. Don't tell me you haven't been thinking of Woodson as the shooter."

I couldn't. "Let's stick to why he'd kill Murray. Would you kill a man you found out was really Amanda's father?"

"I might. To protect Amanda. Woodson had to sincerely believe that Murray was this awful murderer and rapist who's been haunting Garrity all these years. The daughter has to know the story too. It probably gave her

her first nightmares. Woodson killed Murray to protect Bergen from the idea that she was fathered by a monster. If you don't believe that would have kicked her in the head, think about what it's done to Melanie Murray. And she didn't grow up with the Cleveland Circle bogeyman hiding under her bed, like Bergen must have.

"Of course, from what you've told me of Woodson, he might have done it because he was too proud to have the truth about Bergen come out. But let's give him the benefit of the doubt. Let's say he did it for his daughter. He made the appointment to see Murray using Knaff's name. And he killed him."

A nurse who must have barely met the height requirement came in in time to hear Harry's summation. "Who killed who?" she asked.

"Just explaining the plot of a movie I'd seen to my friend here," Harry said easily.

"Well, you'll have to find another place to tell him how it all worked out. We've got your paperwork untangled at last. You're free to go."

What she meant was, Harry was free to begin the process of going. It was after eleven before he'd signed his way out of the building.

Once outside he said, "Where was I?"

"Smoking a cigar on the reservoir, minding your own business."

"Where was I when the nurse walked in on us?"

"You just had Woodson shooting Murray."

"Right. Garrity had found out by then that Murray wasn't the monster after all. But it was too late; Woodson had already executed him. So she switched the hair samples in the police file."

That solution had seemed an easy and obvious action

for Garrity when I'd first thought of it. Now, as Harry casually reasserted the premise, the switch loomed much larger. Potentially, it was the defining moment of Garrity's life. "Why did she run that risk?" I mused aloud.

Harry turned on me. "Are you saying now that Garrity didn't do it? It was your idea in the first place."

"She has to have done it," I said. "I'd just like to understand why."

"You guessed it was to protect whoever had killed Murray. That still works. She didn't want Woodson to know he'd killed an innocent man. As for risk, she had to believe there was no risk. The only one who could know the truth is the real rapist, and she didn't expect him to come forward. The only thing I don't like is the coincidence of Garrity ordering the DNA test at the very moment her husband is stalking poor Murray."

"If it was cause and effect," I said, "there'd be no coincidence. Suppose Garrity ordered the test *because* Woodson had found out about Murray. It forced her hand. She'd been afraid to know the truth until then. By the time she got the results, it was too late."

TWENTY-EIGHT

WE WATCHED a jet pass low over the hospital, a twin of the giant that had ignored our plight the evening before. Then Harry said, "Time to brief the police. You drive, Owen. I'm still feeling a little woozy."

They'd closed two lanes of Commonwealth near the Boston University campus so a crowd of utility workers could stare down into a manhole. As we sat in the resulting traffic jam, I thought back on our struggle in the reservoir. From the comfortable vantage point of a heated leather seat, it seemed like a fiction. I asked Harry how much he remembered of it.

"Not very much. I remember falling in and I remember calling to those cops. Not much in between."

"You called to Mary, too," I said. "You don't remember that?"

"No," Harry answered, flatly and coldly. "Who'd you call to?"

General delivery, I thought, but Harry's point was too plain to laugh away. Whom did I have to call?

We made it through the bottleneck and didn't hit a red light until Berkeley Street. We sat through it in silence. Then, as we were pulling away, Harry said, "Sorry about that crack, Owen. That was a hell of a way to say thanks. Sorry I've been rough on you this whole week. The truth is, I've been a little jealous. Do you believe it?"

I showed him I did by not answering him.

"Mary's mine everywhere else. I mean, in every memory I have of her anywhere but Boston she's either my girl or my fiancée or my wife. But up here, she's your girl. It's stupid, I know, but it's bothered me. You've been feeling the same way, which bothered me even more.

"I've often thought that was why you came back here to hide after you dropped out of the seminary; instead of going home to Jersey, I mean. Because the memory of Mary was here."

It was an interesting insight. I tucked it away and concentrated on my driving. I parked the Lexus in the same garage we'd used on Monday and in almost the same space. Across the street in Government Center's windswept forecourt, they'd fashioned a subway entrance out of the pavement's fancy brick. The sign on the entrance advertised the Green Line, serving Chestnut Hill.

I let Harry get a few steps ahead of me. Then, when he turned to see what was holding me up, I tossed him the car keys. "Give my regards to your cousin."

"Where do you think you're going?"

"Back to the campus. I want to say good-bye to your wife."

"I'm serious, Owen."

"There are things I still have to know. Things the police won't care about."

Harry took a step my way, looked around the crowded plaza, and gave it up. Dignity was a real handicap, I decided. The Harry of old would have chased me down and tackled me, audience or no audience.

"Don't do this, Owen. I promised Amanda I'd look after you."

"I'll stay away from bodies of water."

"I'm not joking. You're not safe. Not with Woodson loose."

This time we both looked around the plaza. "You'd

better get inside," I said. "I'll call Gilder this afternoon to see how you're getting on."

Harry tossed me the keys. "Come by in person," he said.

DESPITE WHAT I'd told Harry, I didn't go straight to the BC campus. I made a stop at Garrity's dark green house in Brookline. I felt safe enough doing it, now that my visit with Corbett had reminded me of the regularity of the academic life. Like Corbett, Wayne Woodson had been keeping office hours on Tuesday. I was counting on him doing the same on this Thursday. That part of my plan worked out; Woodson wasn't in residence in Brookline. But neither was Garrity.

Step two was checking her office in McGuinn Hall, which I reached a little after one o'clock. The office door was shut and locked. As far as I could see, no artificial light was escaping from beneath it. I knocked, but only once or twice. I didn't want my frustration spooking the department secretary, to whom I turned next.

She was already spooked, on the subject of Owen Keane at least. As soon as I asked for Garrity, I saw—in the way the young woman squared her shoulders and the baseball bat grip she took on an innocent ballpoint—that she'd been prepared by Garrity for my likely intrusion.

"The professor is not on campus today," she said, sounding a little less spontaneous than the recording that tells you a number has been disconnected.

"It's very important that I reach her today," I said, in time with the receptionist's head-shaking, which had started as soon as I'd opened my mouth.

"I couldn't possibly give that information out." Not to me.

I didn't press the issue. I was afraid her instructions from Garrity might have included a call to campus security if all else failed.

I left, but didn't go far. I stopped near the stairwell at the end of the hallway to think of a stratagem that might get me a look at the log on the secretary's desk, the log the young woman had pulled toward her protectively when I'd asked for Garrity. The doctor had dutifully signed out on Monday just after Harry and I ambushed her. If she was disciplined enough to do it at that stressful moment, she'd likely done it today. So I had to come up with a way of drawing the log's guardian away.

After ten minutes of concentrated thought, I began to think my hopes hung on the size of the woman's bladder. Then a student brushed past me in the stairwell door. He had hair as long as Stapella's had once been and a jaw so narrow and pointed it made me think of a crocodile's. He wore an unbuttoned flannel shirt over a sweatshirt, a style I couldn't recall from the sixties or any decade since.

"'Scuse me, dude," he said.

"Wait a minute," I said. "How'd you like to make ten bucks?"

"Wow, a whole ten? How about I give you fifteen and you don't bother me anymore?"

"Okay, twenty-five for two minutes work."

"What kind of work?"

"Acting. I want you to go down to Professor Garrity's office. It's the third one past the secretary's desk. Pound on the door and call for her. Make some noise. Don't worry about bothering her. She's not in there."

"Then what's the point?"

"I want you to get the secretary away from her desk for a couple of minutes."

"I say again, dude, what's the point?"

"I want to see her log. I'm a textbook salesman. I have to see Professor Garrity or I won't make a sale. The secretary won't tell me where she is. It's her job to see the professor isn't disturbed. It's my job to disturb her. I play the same game on every campus in my territory."

"Interesting work," the reptile boy said. "Thirty bucks in advance. You'll write it off your taxes, right?"

"Right," I said, thinking that it would make for one interesting audit.

I paid up and he ambled down the hallway. As he passed my adversary's desk, he smiled at her and called her Angel, which I thought an inspired touch. It got her attention and held it. The kid had barely gotten his first I-know-you're-in-there out before she was up and moving.

I moved at the same time, afraid a ringing phone or a squeaking hinge on my end of the hall would draw her attention back to the desk before I could reach it.

My accomplice was spinning a story about a grade that hadn't been turned in, giving me my money's worth and more. I reached the desk and found the log. Next to Garrity's name was printed "Newton campus seminar. One to three."

TWENTY-NINE

UP UNTIL the early sixties, Newton College had been a women's school that was loosely affiliated with Boston College. Once BC went coed, the two schools had slowly merged, after which the Newton campus had become a stepchild, home of a law school and other odds and ends. As an underclassman, I'd heard of students who'd had classes at the satellite, but I'd avoided the inconvenience myself. Still, I knew how to find the place. You couldn't get from the Mass. Pike to Chestnut Hill without passing the campus's gated entrance on Centre Street.

I found the entrance to be not only gated but manned. Two guards were squeezed into a booth built for one, a man my age and his apprentice.

"Morning," the apprentice said to me.

"Afternoon," his mentor whispered.

"I mean, afternoon. Help you?"

I explained that I was looking for Professor Phyllis Garrity. "She's attending a seminar here."

"Here where?" the junior partner asked. "And what seminar?"

"I don't know. I'm from the Lexus dealership. We had her car this morning for service." I patted the steering wheel. Around the same time, I noticed the New Jersey inspection sticker on the windshield. It matched the car's Jersey plates, which the guard might already have noticed. It was too late to change stories, though, so I stumbled on. "Dr. Garrity has our loaner. I'm supposed to hand her her keys and get ours. All they told me was she'd be here at a seminar from one to three."

"We don't—" The kid guard stopped abruptly when his backup began whispering. Then he said, "That'd be Women in Scientific Disciplines. Oates Hall. Make a left and look for the sign. There's a parking lot out front."

Oates Hall looked like a small theater and turned out to be one. Though the outside was as old as the campus— gray square-cut stone, discolored copper gutters, and bronze doors—the inside was new. The auditorium featured a huge dogbone-shaped ceiling panel that must have been installed to correct some deficiency in the acoustics. The reflector was doing its job today. I could hear the speaker quite clearly from my hiding place at the rear of the hall.

What I couldn't begin to do was pick out Garrity's head from the rows of heads before me. I stayed just long enough to convince myself that anyone slipping away early would surely use the back doors. Then I sat down on a lobby bench and waited. To pass the time, I considered how I'd cut Garrity out of a departing crowd if she didn't want to be cut out. I decided I'd stand on my bench and shout the name Seetak Labs until she came to me.

In the end, I didn't have to deal with a crowd or shout code words. When the question-and-answer portion of the program started around two-thirty, the audience began to filter past me in ones and twos. Garrity came out alone. She spotted me right away, her reaction a light-speed combination of shock and resignation that came and went as she took her first step toward me.

She was dressed up today in a black and white checked jacket with pearl buttons and a black skirt. Chic mourning attire, I thought, perhaps for Harry and me.

"Here to take up where we left off?" she asked me,

her voice less alive than the echoes coming from the theater.

I got to my feet, weary, too, suddenly. "Exactly where we left off," I said. "With anger rape. You and anger rape. You didn't just happen upon that specialty. You didn't choose it because no one else had staked a claim or because you felt some sisterly bond with Francine Knaff. The bond you had was with the man you thought had raped Knaff. James Murray."

Garrity ignored the real meat of the charge. "James Murray did rape Francine Knaff. You told me yourself that the police had proved it."

"All they proved was how dangerous it is to let civilians handle their files. You proved Murray wasn't the rapist with your own private DNA test. That ended twenty-six years of agonizing for you over a crime you thought you'd caused."

"I?" Garrity whispered. "I caused Francine Knaff to be raped?"

Even whispered, her question turned heads in what was now a steady stream of departing guests. I took Garrity's arm and led her, unresisting, to the nearest exit. We walked to the western end of the parking lot, where a sundial on a fragment of stone column awaited a break in the overcast.

"Anger rape," I said. "You told me the catalyst is frequently some crisis with an important woman in the rapist's life. A figure of authority. Or a love interest. You were both for Murray. The beautiful older woman who seduced him. You'd tried every way you could to get pregnant by Woodson. Murray was your last resort, a willing student who resembled Woodson. You had him sneaking away from his theater rehearsals and meeting you somewhere on campus. Until you finally conceived. Then you couldn't get rid of him fast enough.''

"He told you that? He talked to you about us?''

"He never told anyone as far as I know. Not even his wife.''

"How, then?'' She answered herself. "You turned out to be a detective after all. The old file was right.'' That was a consolation to her, oddly.

It wasn't to me. "How long before you found out that Murray was the suspect in a horrible rape? How long did you have to be happy about how your scheme had worked out? It can't have been long. I think you cut him loose the very night of the rape. He came back to his rehearsal late that night. And mad, which wasn't like Murray.

"Did you sense right away that you might have set Murray off? Or did that come later, after you'd had time to research causes and effects?''

That was the connection Harry had missed. Garrity wasn't only frightened by the possibility that a rapist and murderer had fathered her child. Her fears were much more specific.

"I'm guessing the real worries started years later, when you'd had time to forget what a sweet guy Murray was, after you'd gotten him tangled up with the rapists you'd read about and interviewed.''

Garrity was willing to let me guess for the moment. She was leaning against the sundial, her supporting hand almost the same gray color as the stone.

"When you sent him away that last night, did he know you were carrying his child? Did you finally tell him what it had all been about?''

"That was the first thing I told him. Before we ever had sex. It was a relief to tell someone about Wayne's obsession to have a child and his inability to father one. I'd been squeezed between those two pincers for so long. I told Jimmy everything. I made him understand what I wanted and made him promise that he wouldn't get involved emotionally, that he'd make no demands of me. He swore he wouldn't."

"But he got involved anyway."

"Yes. I should have known he would. But we had a naive faith back then that we could compartmentalize sex and love. One of our many naive faiths."

"There was an angry scene that last night."

"Yes."

"Where? In your office?"

"I didn't have an office. Jimmy and I met in the office of my faculty advisor, Joshua Ackles. I had a key. Ackles was all but out to pasture. I knew he wouldn't make any after-hours visits. He was rarely there during the day."

Garrity came near to smiling, maybe from picturing those trysts in a dusty office. The impulse faded quickly. "You're right that the idea of Jimmy as the Cleveland Circle murderer crept up on me slowly. I had a terrible shock when I heard he was a suspect, when I realized it had happened only hours after I'd broken things off with him. But it passed. He came by one day to tell me he was innocent. They'd mangled his hair..."

Again a memory distracted her. She waved this one away. "It was the last time I spoke with him before the summer break, the last time until after my maternity leave. I stopped him on campus one day a year or so after our daughter was born. I showed him a picture of Bergen and thanked him. A silly, weak impulse. He was very detached and cool."

Exactly the way a young idiot would act toward the woman he'd lost. I experienced a distracting memory of my own, fleeting pictures of a surprise visit Mary Fitz-gerald had paid to my seminary in Indiana.

Garrity was hurrying on without me. "Still, I wanted to understand what had happened at Cleveland Circle. I had to understand it. I began my serious research on rape, as I told you and Mr. Ohlman. My life's work. Eventu-ally, what I learned convinced me that I knew the identity of the murderer, and that I was an accessory to his crime."

"You were wrong," I said.

"I know that now. But you've known it all along. Since we're being so open with one another, would you mind telling me how you've known?"

She was giving me an opportunity to confess my own guilt. I took advantage of it, almost gratefully. "The rap-ist was a Boston College junior named Alan Avery. He was a transfer student who lived with us at Two Suth-erland Road. I figured it out in 1972, but I never told the police."

"Avery? I don't remember his name from the file." The file she'd pored over the way a fundamentalist stud-ies his Bible, hoping for a glint of salvation. "Why did you keep it to yourself?"

"Avery was dead by seventy-two. He'd volunteered for duty in Vietnam and gotten himself killed there. Prob-ably intentionally."

"You're not afraid I'll reveal his name in my book?"

"I don't think you'll ever finish it. There's no reason for you to now." I made one of my leaps then, this one inspired by Garrity's offer of a chance to confess. "Your book isn't an examination of rape in general or of one brutal attack. It's a confession, isn't it? You were going to name Murray as the rapist and lay out your own in-volvement."

Garrity drew herself up to deny it, but my insights were coming too fast for her. Harry had been quite proud of his solution to the mystery of how Woodson had learned the truth about Bergen's paternity: a sentimental James Murray had walked in one day and told him. I saw now that the truth was simpler by far. "Your husband found out he wasn't Bergen's father by reading your manuscript. You weren't just confessing to your own misjudgment and implicating Murray, you were taking something away from Wayne Woodson he couldn't bear to lose. Did he kill Murray for revenge or to protect Bergen or to make it impossible for you to ever publish the truth?"

Garrity stepped away, putting the sundial column between us. "You can't suspect Wayne."

"We both do. You suspect or you know he killed Murray. You switched the hair samples in the old evidence file so the police would name Murray as the rapist. So your husband would never know he'd killed an innocent man."

She leaned toward me across the stone column, her ashen hands small fists. "You have to forget all this, Mr. Keane. You're not empowered to interfere, whatever might have happened when you were a student. You're not equipped to handle this. Leave it to me, please. No good can come of making this public. You can't bring back Jimmy. If there were a way to do that, I'd have done it myself. If it meant giving up my own life, I'd have done it.

"You can't bring about any good, but you can do terrible harm. Wayne and I have a daughter. She's Wayne's no matter who her biological father might be. You have to believe that. Bergen would be devastated by the theories you're tossing about. You don't want that. Jimmy wouldn't want it either."

"Murray had a second daughter," I said. "Melanie's already been devastated by that newspaper clipping Woodson left on her father's corpse. A clipping that came from your own private scrapbook on Cleveland Circle. It'll be ten times worse for Melanie when the police DNA tests are made public.

"You can't ignore the truth, Phyllis. Not for Bergen's sake or any other reason. No good will come of that. I know. I said just now that I didn't tell the police about Alan Avery in 1972 because he was dead. But there was more to it. I went to see Avery's mother. My friend Harry and I went to see her. In Needham, where she lived."

Though badly distracted, Garrity was still a scientist. "What was she like?"

"Younger than I expected. Younger looking. Like no classmate's mother I'd ever met. Sexy. Dressed like the girls on campus dressed.

"Her house was very modern, too. Very nice. I was intimidated by the place, but luckily I had Harry along. I'd worked out a little scene for us to play, and Harry had the biggest part."

"I don't understand."

"I thought I knew what had happened that night at Cleveland Circle. And afterward. But I wasn't sure. I intended to trick Mrs. Avery. She'd given her son his alibi. So she had to know what he'd done.

"I had Harry tell her that he'd received a letter from Vietnam. From Avery. The letter was a confession to the sixty-nine murder, to be used by Harry in the event the police arrested an innocent man. And I had Avery tell Harry in the letter that he didn't intend to come back from the war alive."

"Why did Mr. Ohlman receive the letter in your fiction? Why not you?"

"Harry's whole family are lawyers. I thought it would sound more believable for Avery to choose someone like Harry who could keep tabs on the case."

"Did the lie work?"

"Yes. Mrs. Avery broke down. She told us her son had come home to Needham that night to spend the weekend as planned. But he hadn't stayed. She'd spoiled the weekend by telling Alan that she and Alan's father were getting a divorce. He'd caught her with another man. A younger man, not much older than Alan. She said Alan took the news badly. 'Agitated' was the word she used to describe his reaction. I asked her if Alan had gotten drunk before he left her."

"He hadn't," Garrity said, putting her years of research to work. "But his anger was very like drunkenness. Did she say it changed him? That she didn't know him?"

"Yes, I think she did use the word *stranger* to describe him. She thought he might have only been gone for an hour. Certainly no more than two. When he came back, he was dazed, and his clothes were splattered with blood."

"And Mrs. Avery didn't call the police."

"No. The cover-up started with her. She never even told her husband. She ended up pleading with Harry and me to keep the secret with her. She used your argument. We couldn't bring the victim back. We couldn't even punish Avery, since he'd beaten us to it. We could only blacken his name and punish the people he'd tried to protect.

"She swore that Harry would never have to use the

confession. She promised that if anyone was arrested for the murder, she'd come forward herself."

"Did you believe her?"

"Yes. She claimed she would have come forward to save an innocent man even if her son were still alive. I didn't believe that."

"She didn't come forward when Jimmy was killed," Garrity said. "Why not?"

"She killed herself three years ago. Driving drunk. She'd remarried several times. The last name she had was Timony.

"In the end, Harry and I agreed to keep her secret. We were playing God, though we didn't think of it that way. We put protecting people and reputations and relationships ahead of the truth. By doing that, we condemned James Murray to death."

Garrity had caught the feeling of my story; tears were streaming down her face. But she'd missed the moral. "Let it end with Jimmy. Please. I promise you it will."

'It's too late for it to end with Jimmy. Someone shot at Harry and me last night. It's still going, Phyllis. It'll go on until the truth comes out."

Garrity was backing away from me. "I started this," she said. "I can stop it. I'm the only one who can."

THIRTY

I WATCHED GARRITY go without saying another word. I watched her back away from me and then hurry to her car, which wasn't a Lexus or anything like one. Then I watched the empty space where the car had been.

I was distracted at that critical moment by memories of Mrs. Avery that I hadn't shared with Garrity. I'd ended the long-ago interview in Needham by departing from my carefully prepared outline. I'd surprised both Mrs. Avery and Harry by asking her if her dead son had ever studied for the priesthood. She'd told me that Avery had started down that long road as an undergraduate at Mount St. Mary's. She'd also passed on a warning, though I hadn't recognized it as one at the time. She'd said that the priesthood hadn't been Alan's idea. It had been planted in his mind by others.

The ticking of the sundial finally roused me. Or the cracking sound the overcast made as it broke apart did. The sun shone down, too late in the day to warm me. Too late in general.

I managed to walk to Harry's car and get it started. As soon as I did, its phone began to ring. The caller was Harry, who had either gotten lucky on his first try or had been sending messages into the ether every five minutes. It was door number two, if Harry's aggrieved tone was any indication.

"Events are leaving you behind, Owen," he said.

"That's my feeling, too," I replied.

I'd gotten as far as shifting the car into drive. I dropped it into park again as Harry asked, "Are you okay?"

"Yes."

"My cousin's wearing his seven-league boots today. His people have already discovered that a car registered to Wayne Woodson was ticketed for illegal parking on Chestnut Hill Avenue last night. Near one of the reservoir gates. The gate was locked, of course, but anyone reasonably active could climb it. You probably could."

"Not today," I said.

"Their background check on Woodson also turned up a gun registration. A thirty-eight revolver the police are anxious to test."

They weren't as anxious to test it as I was for them to have it somewhere safe. "What else?"

"Harry got a report from the Dominion Hotel about the messages we found on our suite computer."

"They were entered on a lobby terminal by person or persons unknown, right?"

"No. They were sent from another room in the hotel. Room 1313."

"The Dominion doesn't have a thirteenth floor," I said.

"Exactly. Does that make any sense to you?"

"Only poetic sense. Anything else?"

"No. It'll take time to verify that oral history you picked up about Woodson and Garrity's conception problems, if it can be verified at all."

A teenage pedestrian started to walk in front of the Lexus, then paused and waved me out of the parking space. I waved to her to go ahead. We waved back and forth for a time, then she walked around behind me. I checked my reflection in the vanity mirror and decided I didn't blame her for being cautious. I looked that burnt out.

"Did you hear me, Owen?"

"Garrity's already admitted that she slept with Murray."

"You've spoken to her? Owen, the police are looking for Woodson right now. If Garrity passes on some warning from you and he gets away, you'll be in serious trouble."

Not the least of which would be the sore neck I'd get from looking over my shoulder for the rest of my life.

"Did she admit that Woodson killed Murray?" Without waiting for an answer, Harry turned the question into a further indictment. "It wouldn't have mattered if she had admitted it, since you probably forgot to bring a witness along and you certainly weren't wearing the wire Harry would have given you if you'd let him know what you were up to."

"In my business, we walk on wires," I said. "We don't wear them."

"Right now you're working without a net."

"Touché. I think Garrity may talk Woodson into turning himself in. She thinks she's the only one who can stop this, since she started it."

"And all this time we've been thinking we started it," Harry said. "Or do we still think that?"

"We did our part," I said.

"Well, we're out of it now. Get down here, Owen. Don't make us come and get you."

"I'm on my way. One last stop and I'll be there."

Harry was drawing breath to object when I pressed a button on the phone. It was marked, succinctly, End.

I SAW THE SAME security tag team as I left the Newton campus, but didn't stop to tell them any more bedtime stories. I drove down Commonwealth to BC's main entrance and found a parking space ready and waiting for me. Leaving the car and its troublesome phone behind, I walked up the broad avenue between St. Mary's Hall and Bapst Library. It ended in a little traffic circle in front of ancient Gasson. At the grassy center of this circle was a tall marble column and atop the column, a gilded statue of a wingspread eagle.

I'd heard once that the statue had been a gift to the college from the Japanese ambassador to the United States, though I'd never inquired after his interest in the school. More intriguing to me had been a campus legend connected with the golden bird. It said that if a virgin ever graduated from Boston College, the eagle would flap its wings and fly away.

Thanks to Mary Fitzgerald, I'd graduated without putting that legend to the test. So it was appropriate that we'd chosen the eagle column as our rendezvous point on our graduation day, a place where we could escape our families for a few private moments. Now I was standing in the shadow of the column again, drawn there by something I'd recently said. It wasn't the promise I'd made to Harry about saying good-bye to his wife, though that was in the back of my mind. The prod was something I'd told Garrity. My stirring declaration that the truth was more important than people and relationships.

The eagle column had been a poor choice for a tryst, as every third member of our class had decided to be photographed in front of it. I was asked to photograph more than one happy family myself while I waited for Mary, and I surely appeared in the background of many other pictures, a lone figure scanning the crowd. When Mary finally appeared, we paced Bapst's backyard, walking up and down in front of a line of severely trimmed old crab trees that were still in bloom. We'd both passed our mortarboards and diplomas to willing relations, which freed up our hands. Even so, we didn't use them to touch one another.

Did I think back on my interview with Mrs. Avery during that last walk? The visit to Needham and the good-bye I said to Mary seemed like cause and effect to me now, but did I spot the relationship at the time? Did I see that the idea of trying the seminary myself—just the germ of an idea at graduation—had been passed to me by Avery, himself an unwilling carrier? I couldn't remember.

Nor could I clearly recall how Mary's face had looked that day. I could picture the old crab trees, gone now, replaced by a gated access road for the new library. I paced the road where the trees had stood, trying to visualize Mary and failing.

I wanted to remember that I'd told her all about the promise I'd made to Avery's mother and how that compromise had made me fearful of other, larger compromises. I wanted to remember that I'd told Mary of the challenge Avery had thrown down before me: take my questioning more seriously—gamble my life on finding my answers—or give up the search, the way he had. Being the author of my memories, I should have been able to whip up that dialogue easily, as I'd been doing all week.

I was kept from doing it by the certain knowledge that I hadn't told Mary those things. And by the fear that I'd left her thinking that our parting was somehow her fault.

I didn't have Harry with me to whistle appropriate background music, but I heard some nevertheless. It was "Dedicated to the One I Love," the old Mamas and Papas hit I'd imagined playing on the radio when I'd reconstructed the night Mary cut my hair on the porch at Two Sutherland. The tune, at once driving and sentimental, came through clearly now, but I only caught the lyrics in snatches. One was about a little prayer being something everybody needs.

And then I did remember Mary's face, older-looking in its careful graduation-day makeup, her blue eyes smiling at me, willing me to smile back. And I could hear her running on and on about a job she'd taken with IBM, filling the silence I should have put to better use.

The image came and went before I had time to say good-bye or anything else.

THIRTY-ONE

BEFORE I PULLED the Lexus into traffic, I unplugged the telephone. At the rate Gilder was moving, I was afraid I'd be told next that Woodson had been convicted and sentenced to hard labor upstate. I didn't want to hear that the case was finished for everyone else when it was still so far from finished for me.

I was thinking again about the attack at the reservoir. That was natural enough, since I was in the neighborhood, the Dominion Hotel slipping by on my right. I slowed the car and began to look for a parking space, feeling that I'd used up my luck parking at the college. I was almost to Cleveland Circle before I found a slot big enough.

I climbed back up the hill to the reservoir gate that Harry had pronounced easy to climb. I would have challenged him to demonstrate, if he'd been handy. The iron gate, green where it wasn't rusted, had pointed uprights and awkwardly placed crossbars, one too low to be much good and the other almost too high to reach.

So much for the gate. I followed the green iron fence attached to the gate, moving to my right, up the hill and into the trees. The fence rose as the ground did, but a dozen yards from the gate, I found a place where the ground rose much faster, aided by a sudden outcropping of quartz-flecked gray rock around which the fence had been forced to detour. Standing on the rock, I could put one foot on the upper crossbar of the fence with only moderate strain on the tendons of my legs and the seams of my trousers. I pushed off with the leg that was still braced against the rock, clearing the fence's rusty tines and coming down on the other side, more or less feet first.

I looked around for some sign that Woodson had made the same leap—in the dark, no less. The wooded hillside was beyond the area policed by the Dominion's staff, so there was no shortage of material. I found junk food wrappers, plastic soda bottles, and beer cans. When I came across the first spent condom, I decided that sifting through the physical evidence could safely be left to the official police.

I backtracked to the disused path that went through the padlocked gate. Then, in defiance of my promise to Harry that I'd stay away from bodies of water, I followed the path down to the reservoir circuit. For the first time, I saw the lake as I remembered it, without halogen lighting or a foreground of luxury hotel. Just the gray water, kicked up by the wind, the setting sun glinting off the tiny wave tops.

The point on the jogging track where Harry had been enjoying his cigar was just below me. That it was near the path that led to the corner of the property where Woodson had parked his car had been a happy coincidence for the English professor. As Gilder had said, Woodson had needed only to find a place from which he could see most of the walk and then finalize his arrangements after Harry had come to rest. Harry had made the job easy by coming right to him.

Or rather, I had made the job easy for Woodson. Because Harry hadn't really picked the spot where he'd smoke his cigar. I had, in 1972, on the day Steven Stapella had told me about Avery's extra key. I'd come back from the combat zone drunk and parked as near as I could to the reservoir gate I knew from our Cleveland Circle days. I'd walked through the gate, which was unlocked back then, followed the path to the water, and sat down to cry my drunken tears. Harry had found me there later, the event marking the site indelibly for him. When he'd read the phony message summoning him to a meeting on the reservoir path, he'd naturally walked to that old shrine, the way I'd gravitated toward my private landmarks all week.

So what had appeared to be a lucky break from the shooter's point of view really wasn't, when seen from Harry's viewpoint or mine. But that left another coincidence unexplained. Why had Woodson chosen the reservoir in the first place?

I could hear the Harrys' answer. The reservoir had been convenient to the hotel and the ideal spot for the ambush, with maximum cover and minimum witnesses. End of discussion.

I ran the answer by myself several times but never felt satisfied. The reservoir *was* the perfect place from the shooter's perspective. The nagging problem was that it was also the perfect place from the shootees' perspective. From Harry's and mine. It was the very place either one of us would have chosen for a talk, convenient and private, yes, but also significant in a way only the two of us would have known.

Then I remembered a third person in all of Boston who knew the significance of the reservoir to Harry and me. Melanie Murray. I'd told her of it myself, during our impromptu lunch in the hotel café. I'd explained my inattention by saying that the nearby reservoir had been an important landmark for Harry and me. That was all I'd told her, but it might have been enough.

As I considered the unlikely idea, I unconsciously be-

gan to walk toward the hotel, the only place I'd ever seen
Melanie. I didn't get far. I told myself that I shouldn't
leave the reservoir without verifying the second part of
Harry's hypothesis. I'd proven that a gunman could have
gotten in over the fence from the street side. But could
he have gotten out again?

Could *she* have gotten out again? I might as well have
phrased it that way, because I'd begun to think in terms
of a much younger, shorter sniper. This time I searched
downhill from the gate. I found a path many small feet
had made in the underbrush and followed it. It led me to
a hole in the fence: one missing vertical post with the
posts on either side of the gap bent away slightly. The
resulting opening was too small for me to slip through.
Too small for Woodson, too, which may have been why
Gilder's scouts had ignored it. It was just wide enough
for the neighborhood kids and maybe for a woman who
wasn't much older.

I returned to the reservoir path and hurried to the hotel,
not drawing a second glance from today's stair machine
pilots as I entered the workout room. I climbed to the
lobby, scanned it for Melanie, and checked for messages
from the thirteenth floor at a public terminal, which is to
say, I wasted my time. Then I left the Dominion through
the front door and followed the sidewalk down to the
waiting sedan.

I knew from Harry's background lectures that the Mur-
rays lived in Arlington, north and west of Cambridge.
Harry knew the exact address, I was sure, but he wasn't
likely to tell me unless I agreed to take him along. I liked
him better where he was.

I found a street map of Boston where I knew my me-
thodical partner would have one, in his glove compartment, tucked under the warranty card for his tires. I used

the map to cut through Brighton and to find the Larz
Anderson Bridge across the Charles. I blundered then,
taking Route 2A through the center of Cambridge when
2 would have let me skirt it. I didn't have the leisure time
to see that on the map until I was stuck in the evening
traffic around Harvard University. Then I had time
enough to draw my own map.

My luck reversed itself when I finally made it to Arlington. The drugstore where I stopped to borrow a phone
book turned out to be only a block away from the address
the book gave me for J. C. Murray.

The Murray house was an old but well-kept brick two-
story with an enclosed front porch that still held a hint
of warmth from the sun's last-minute appearance. That
was more than could be said of Rita Murray's greeting
when she opened the front door.

She'd been home from work long enough to untuck
her blouse from her skirt and lose her shoes. Her blond
hair was drawn back and tied somehow, which might
have been another sign that she was off the clock. She
looked tired, but she was still young enough for it to seem
a temporary condition. She blocked the open doorway
with her body, chest thrust toward me in what would
have been an attractive pose if there'd been anything re-
motely friendly in her expression.

"I thought I asked you not to come here," she said.

"You did. I wouldn't have come if it hadn't been important."

"Has something happened to Harry?"

I looked for some sign that she returned Harry's nas-
cent interest in her. Her face told me less than her comfortable use of his first name had. Still, I thought, it might
be a way to get me off the porch.

"Someone took a shot at him last night." I didn't add

that the same person had shot at me, since Rita seemed to be considering that option herself.

"Is he okay?"

"He spent the night in the hospital, but he's okay now. He's with the police at the moment."

"Do they think it was the same person who shot Jim?"

"Yes, they do." I was less sure of my own opinion.

"You'd better come in, then."

She sat me down in a living room that reminded me of the one I'd left behind when I entered Boston College. Furniture worn to the point of fraying, carpet showing the traffic pattern as clearly as a fresh snow, painted plaster walls that had been inexpertly stripped of their wallpaper, the little gouges left by the scrapers visible where the light from the turned-pine table lamp hit them just right. It was a room that could change its role on demand, like the inside of a camper. A television room certainly, but a dining room, too, when the folded TV tables in the corner were brought into use. I was willing to bet that the sofa on which Rita sat transformed itself like a kid's toy when an extra bedroom was needed. At the moment, the room was the place where unwanted visitors were received.

"How did it happen?" Rita asked.

I gave her a bare outline of the prior evening's excitement. She grew so puzzled as I talked that I stopped well short of our ride in the ambulance.

"All that over an audit?" she asked.

"We're here for more than an audit, Mrs. Murray. Didn't Harry hint at that during your lunch?"

"Our lunch? We didn't have lunch, Mr. Keane. We went to the Parker House Hotel and fucked each other's brains loose. He kept asking if he could do anything for me. That's what I wanted. I'd had my fill of having my hand patted. I wanted sex with someone who wasn't going to bother me later.''

She lit a cigarette, savoring her first drag and my reaction to her little bombshell. ''Harry said you shocked easily.''

I also bounced back quickly. ''He didn't tell you that we'd come up here to look into your husband's murder?''

''No.''

''That's why we were shot at last night. We're getting close to the truth.''

''And you've come here to tell me what you've found?'' She kept the cigarette in her mouth as she asked, a trick I'd never mastered.

''I've come to talk to your daughter.''

''To Melanie? She's the reason I asked you to stay away from here.''

''Melanie contacted me, Mrs. Murray. At the Dominion Hotel. Otherwise I would have respected your wishes. She was desperate to know the truth about her father.''

''Melanie already has her truth. Her father was a rapist. It's her excuse to make a damn mess of her life and she's determined to use it. And you've been trying to help her behind my back? Tell me, was it the same way Harry helped me at the Parker House?''

I waited until her anger had faded a little before I said, ''No.''

''I'm sorry. I shouldn't take things out on you. How did Melanie even know you were here?''

''She said you told her about talking to us on Monday. She came to see me that same night.''

''I never spoke to her about you, Mr. Keane. Why would I? The last thing I wanted was Melanie stirred up again.''

"You must have mentioned it. She knew all about the audit."

Rita searched her memory while I moved on to larger doubts. "Was Melanie away from home on Monday night?"

"She's away from home every night. She's away right now."

"How about Tuesday at lunch time? Could she have slipped away from school?"

"No. She got in trouble Tuesday morning. For fighting. She was being held in the principal's office at lunch time. The message was waiting for me when I got back from seeing Harry."

I felt as though I were in a reservoir again, the black water closing over me. "May I see a picture of Melanie? A recent one."

"I have her yearbook picture. It was taken last summer. Melanie hates it, so I can't have it out. But I like it. It reminds me of the way things used to be for us. And it's a good likeness, whatever Melanie thinks."

She crossed to a badly scarred secretary and returned with a blue cardboard folder. It contained an eight-by-ten of a smiling, nicely tanned young woman whom I'd never met. A young Rita Murray, from her golden hair on down.

THIRTY-TWO

I LEFT RITA MURRAY without an explanation or a fare-well, only pausing at the glass door of her porch to scan the dark street. The Lexus was where I'd left it, and I ran to it. Once safely locked inside, I fumbled with the car phone, trying to restore it to life without using the dome light. When I finally did, I punched in Gilder's number, pulling the sedan into traffic as the policeman's phone rang.

A woman's voice I didn't recognize answered with the abbreviated title of his office. "Police Liaison."

I asked for Gilder.

"And you are?"

"Owen Keane."

"He left his cell phone number for you."

She read it off. I pictured every digit so I'd have a slight hope of remembering them. The technique worked. Gilder answered the new number himself.

"It's Keane," I said. "Where are you?"

Wherever he was, he was too busy to deal with me. Harry came on immediately. "Owen, are you all right?"

"Yes. Where are you guys?"

"Brookline. Phyllis Garrity's house. She was shot this evening."

"Dead?"

"Not at the last report. But she's in bad shape. If one of Harry's teams hadn't come by here looking for Wood-son, she'd be even worse. They haven't found him yet, by the way. Woodson."

"He may be lying shot somewhere himself," I said.

"If this were a murder-suicide, he'd have shot himself right here. He wouldn't have gone off to hide."

"Woodson didn't shoot Garrity. He didn't shoot Murray either. We've been wrong, Harry. Garrity wasn't protecting her husband when she switched the samples. She was protecting her daughter. Murray's daughter. Bergen."

"How—"

"Bergen's the one who came by to see me. Not Melanie Murray. I mistook her for Melanie, and she went along with it."

She'd said, "You talked to my mother today," at our first meeting, and I'd pictured Rita Murray, the woman with the damaged daughter, forgetting the other mother we'd spoken to that day, Garrity. We'd fed Garrity our audit cover story, and she'd passed it on to Bergen. Why Garrity had done it, I couldn't guess.

Harry said, "I thought Bergen was working in New York."

"So did I. We'll find out now she quit or took a leave of absence sometime before Murray was killed. She's been in Boston all this time."

"Where are you, Owen?"

"Leaving Arlington. I was having second thoughts about Melanie. I came out here to talk with her. She wasn't home, but her mother showed me her picture."

"So you're thinking Bergen found out the truth about Murray and killed him?"

"Not the whole truth. That he was her real father, yes, but not that he was innocent of the Cleveland Circle rape. Bergen was the one Garrity was trying to head off with that DNA test. You got one part of it right: Garrity must have poisoned her daughter's life with her fears about the old rape."

Harry wasn't anxious to claim the idea. "Is that why Bergen shot her mother? For poisoning her life?"

"Or for insisting that Bergen give herself up. Garrity told me she was going to end it. Maybe Bergen wasn't ready to."

That prompted us both to meditate on Bergen's unfinished business. The interlude lasted long enough to get me through the next light. Then Harry said, "Are you coming here? Because I'm not sure how much longer we'll be here ourselves. Maybe you should go straight to Gilder's office."

And lock myself in his upper right-hand desk drawer. "I'm going back to the Dominion," I said. I knew Harry would want a reason, so I slipped him a beauty. "Gilder's going to blame me for what happened to Garrity. I'm too tired to face that tonight."

"Good idea. If your tip on Bergen pans out in the meantime, it'll balance the scales."

"I'm hoping they'll balance," I said.

I restrained an impulse to tell him to take care of himself or to ask him to remember me to Amanda or to say anything else that would let him know how jumpy I was.

But I couldn't let him go away empty-handed. "Rita sends her love, Harry."

"Damn it, Owen," Harry said, and broke the connection.

I HANDED OVER my borrowed sedan to the Dominion's staff with real regret. I told the aging bellhop who took the keys that it needed gas—a little amber likeness of a gas pump had glowed beneath the speedometer all the way back from Arlington. I thought I was requesting a feedbag for a faithful mount. He thought I was making a joke and faked a laugh.

The lobby jungle was unusually crowded and the natives were unusually well dressed. Some formal affair was getting underway in the hotel's ballroom, I gathered. As protective cover went, the black tie and evening gown crowd was of little use to me. I would have blended as well with a synchronized swim team. But they were company. When my personal contingent left our elevator car at the mezzanine where the ballroom was located, I felt the loss.

I'd yet to see another resident of the tenth floor in the hallway and I didn't see one tonight. I looked for and found the smoked glass dome that hid the security camera and smiled at it nervously. I would have waved at it, too, but my arms seemed fastened to my sides. It was all I could do to raise one high enough to slip my electronic key into the lock.

The paralysis spread once I managed to get the door open. Walking into the dark suite was like waking in the night to the imagined sound of someone in my room, a phenomenon I tortured myself with regularly. I felt a familiar inability to turn my head on my neck. Not that it mattered. It was too late to be watching my step.

Enough light was coming in through the picture window for me to navigate around the furniture and reach the center of the main room. Once there, I stopped and forced myself to swallow.

"Where are you, Bergen?" I asked, my voice a little loud, but otherwise okay.

"Right here."

The lights came on in the bulkhead above the bar, and she stepped from behind it, for once without her pea jacket. It wouldn't have gone very well with her ensemble, a mustard-colored blouse of washed silk and a silk skirt that was a swirl of purples and browns with accents of the yellow. The pale slender figure had more in common with the glittering couples I'd dropped at the mezzanine than with the young woman I'd mistaken for Melanie Murray.

Her hands were at her sides, her right one hidden by the generous cut of her skirt. I tried not to fixate on that hidden hand.

It was my turn to say something. I came up with "You clean up nice."

"I had to," Bergen said. "They won't rent a suite to just anybody. I'm surprised they let you up here dressed like that."

"You have one of the suites?"

"The one next door. I've had it since Tuesday."

"Is that how you got in here? Did you cut your way in through the linen closet?"

"Guess again."

I wouldn't have bothered, except that she was grinning and the grin was scaring me more than her hidden right hand. I'd expected to find her waiting for me, but I'd also expected her to be broken down over what she'd done to her mother, someone I could reach by consoling and explaining and generally making things right.

Now I wondered if I'd ever really worked that last trick in all my years of trying. And I wondered if Bergen was the one I'd really come to help. Harry's mention of balancing the scales had focused a vague feeling I'd had since my visit to the eagle column, an idea that my whole wandering life might be viewed as a reaction to the Cleveland Circle tragedy. I'd seen the case as wrapped up when I'd left Mrs. Avery in 1972, but it hadn't been. Now there was another chance. The realization brought with it the crazy notion that if the cycle finally did end, I might find myself safely back on the solid rails I'd jumped after graduation.

"Guess," Bergen prompted, but not impatiently.

"You're a computer expert. You got around the security system somehow."

"I'm an editor of computer manuals. Not a techno-geek. The only thing I've learned about computer systems is that they're no better than the people who run them. No system is. Take this hotel's electronic key system. Its weak link is the man behind the lobby desk. If a nicely dressed young hotel guest, one who's stopped by to flirt with him once or twice, tells him she's locked her key in her suite, he might format a new one for her without checking to see that she'd given him the right suite number."

"You're being too modest. You know computers. You figured out how to hack your way into the hotel's message system. You left a message to Harry from a non-existent room. And you knew when he'd deleted it. You had to have monitored that somehow because you typed it back in.

"Were you in Brookline when I came by to see your mother last night? Is that why you shot at us? Or was it just our time to go?"

"I saw you there. I hurried back here and left the message for Mr. Ohlman. I was afraid you wouldn't get back in time, but you did. Barely. I'd already scouted the reservoir. I'd found how I could get back in there without being seen from the hotel."

"Why did you reenter the message Harry had deleted? Why didn't you just leave me one from him?"

"Psychology. From what I knew of Mr. Ohlman, I was sure he'd take the message at face value. I was just as sure you wouldn't. So I gave you one you could see through.''

"How did you know I wouldn't send the police out after Harry?"

"How did I know Harry so well?" she asked, stating the question I'd overlooked. "I've never met him, remember?"

"You studied the old case file. You believed in it, the way your mother did. You're her daughter after all."

"I'm my father's daughter," Bergen said and raised the gun she'd been hiding, a stainless steel revolver. "The daughter of a rapist and a murderer. Bad news for you."

"James Murray never raped anyone."

"That's what my mother told me tonight. After she said she'd sent my...her husband someplace far away to delay the police. To give me time to give myself up. She said Murray wasn't the rapist. But I'd already read the truth in her manuscript. I found it when I came home last Christmas. I recognized my old bedtime story, the Cleveland Circle rape. And guess what? I found out I was the cause of it. My conception was its conception. We're all conceived in sin, they tell us, but I overdid it. My father was a man who beat women to death for foreplay. Imagine what reading that by the glow of the Christmas tree was like."

She gave me a glimpse of that night. Tears began to course down her face until her cheeks were glistening with them. I could almost see the reflection of multicolored lights.

"I didn't sleep through the night again until I realized that I had to avenge Francine Knaff. I was the one woman in the world custom-made for the job. I tracked Murray down and got an appointment to see him using Francine's name."

"The appointment was for a Mr. Knaff."

"You're looking at his secretary. I borrowed the gun my mother's husband kept and went to see Murray."

"Did you tell him who you were?"

"No. I'd planned to. I had a whole speech memorized. I wanted him to know that I was doing it for Francine and for all women. But I never got to say anything. He'd been drinking, I think. He started to yell for help as soon as he saw the gun. I panicked and shot him. I hadn't been sure I'd be able to, right up until I pulled the trigger. Then I pulled it and pulled it and pulled it."

That reminded her of something. "My mother screamed tonight when she saw the gun. I told her I'd thrown it away, but she came charging in and said she knew I hadn't, that I'd used it again last night. I wasn't going to shoot her, but she started to scream."

"Your mother's still alive," I said. "The police found her in time."

For a second Bergen bought it. But she was Woodson's daughter, too, someone for whom the temptation to believe was quicksand. "That's another lie. You lie to make people feel better. It's a weakness of yours. You lied when you told me that James Murray wasn't the rapist. You thought that would make me feel better."

I remembered how she'd taken that news: like the lifeline I was throwing her was a snake. It was the last thing she'd wanted to hear. The last thing she'd believe.

"Why did you come to the hotel that first night? It wasn't to pretend to be Melanie Murray. I put that idea in your head."

Bergen nodded. "You offered me that out and I took it. I told myself it would give me more time to size up things, but I was just being weak. I came to you to find out what you knew and what I had to do next."

"Don't you mean, who you had to kill next?"

"Yes," Bergen said very quietly. "Who I had to kill next."

"Were you thinking of us as targets then, Harry and me? Or were you already planning to silence your mother?"

"I only shot her because she panicked when she saw the gun. I didn't mean to, even though she deserved it as much as he did. She raped Murray. Seduced him and used him. She said so in her manuscript. Her formula went like this: I raped my student and he raped a nurse. That was her big confession, that's why rape obsessed her. Why I grew up with it underfoot like the nasty old family pet. Why I've never been touched by a man without thinking of it. We're all conceived in rape, Mr. Keane. That's what it comes down to. That's why we do such terrible things to each other."

Her tears had passed as suddenly as they'd come on. "Murray panicked, too, when he saw the gun," she said with academic detachment. "You're the first one who's stood there like it's no big deal. Have you watched too many cop shows on TV? No. This has happened to you before, hasn't it?"

"Yes," I said.

She nodded to herself. "Because of your hobby. Poking your nose into things. How many times? Once or twice? More?"

"More."

"I can't have you bored, Mr. Keane. I can't have you certain you know how this will end, either. I'll have to think of some twist to hold your interest."

She straightened her gun arm, thrusting the revolver

toward me. "I could shoot you right now. That would be a twist. But I might kill you. Then you wouldn't be able to tell the police what happened here. And why I did what I did."

She drew the gun back, tucking it close to her chest and pushing the barrel up into the soft flesh beneath her jaw. "Bet you've never seen this one," she said.

"Wait!" I said, stepping toward her without thinking.

"Get back! Get back or you'll have blood all over you!"

Now I understood why she'd come to the Dominion that first night—feverish and desperate. She'd been thinking of taking her own life ever since she'd killed Murray. She'd come to me to find out if her time was up.

"I already have blood all over me," I said. "James Murray's blood. I knew who raped Francine Knaff and I kept quiet about it. The rapist was dead by the time I figured it out. I didn't think it would do anyone any good to tell. I didn't know what your mother was going through or what it would do to you.

"Please don't make it worse for everyone by hurting yourself. What started that night in 1969 has to end now. More violence won't end it.

"You don't want to kill yourself, Bergen, any more than you really tried to kill Harry and me last night. You wanted to scare us off. You fired your last shot in the air, didn't you? Everything you've done here at the hotel has been a stall, like taking Melanie's name."

I dried up then, just when I had to hold her attention. I told myself to say anything, but keep talking. "Your mother said today that vengeance was the last thing James Murray would want. She was right. It's the last thing she wants. She'll tell you that herself if you ask her."

"How did the rapist die?"

"He took his own life. He couldn't face up to what he'd done. If he'd been able to, all our lives would have been different. I had the chance to tell the truth and I let it go by. It doesn't matter that I'd do it differently today. My chance is past forever. This is *your* chance, Bergen. My telling the police what you did and why won't save us. Your telling them will."

She was crying again. I held my hand out for the gun. Neither of us heard a key go into the lock of the suite or the bolt draw back. The door opened and Harry walked in, Gilder a step behind him. Harry froze when he saw us, but his cousin reached for the gun on his belt.

Bergen had turned toward the sound of the door. She turned back to me now, her eyes wide and bottomless. She opened her mouth to scream as Murray and Garrity had.

I raised my outstretched hand. "Save us, Bergen. Please."

THIRTY-THREE

I⟨T WAS A⟩ beautiful afternoon, the first really warm one since we'd gotten to Boston. Because of the fine weather, we'd elected to eat outside, Rebecca Wiese and I. We were seated on opposite sides of a round metal table. It had a glass top that was smooth on our side but textured on the bottom, either for visual interest or to obscure our view of each other's knees. The texturing mimicked the surface of the glistening reservoir, just beyond the deck on which we sat. Looking through the glass was like lying at the bottom of the lake, staring up at the world.

Rebecca was discussing DNA again, though she looked like anything but a lecturer in her white sun dress and broad-brimmed white hat. More like a bridesmaid. No, I amended, letting myself sink a little in my chair. More like a bride.

"It's in the polymorphic regions," she was saying. "You remember them, don't you?"

"The stretches of DNA you haven't been able to map," I said, hoping to cut the lecture short. "The ones that are different for each person. The mystery code."

"The mystery code," Rebecca repeated, smiling and nodding, the brim of her hat making the motion a playful wave. "How apt a phrase in your case. It's in there."

"What is?" I asked, afraid I'd missed the point somehow with my contemplation of the tabletop.

"The explanation for your obsession with mystery, for your searching after answers. And for your inability to accept any compromise to your search, which, I may say, includes most aspects of a normal life.

"You think an impulsive decision you made in 1972 shaped your destiny—a very romantic notion. You think a promise of silence forced out of you by a grieving mother led to your ill-conceived plan to take up where her son had left off. You're afraid now that you tried to become a priest to undo his failure in some symbolic and superstitious way. Instead of which, you repeated his fall."

How much had I told her and why? In my embarrassment and confusion, I couldn't remember. I looked down at the table before me expecting to see ice cubes melting in a glass that had recently held scotch. A lot of scotch. Instead I saw a teacup without so much as a tea leaf on its dry bottom.

"I wasn't trying to become Avery," I said. "I wanted answers."

"About God and the universe and Owen Keane," Rebecca said, her hat waving at me again. "It doesn't matter what you *thought* you were doing. That's what I'm here to tell you. It doesn't even matter if you had a plausible subconscious reason. Or a hundred. The real cause predates your consciousness. The real reason you are who you are is your mystery code."

"Is it?"

"Of course. So you can forget that odd idea you have that solving Murray's murder, laying the old ghosts of Cleveland Circle, will somehow straighten out your life. That's never going to happen."

"It isn't?"

"Don't be sad, Owen. Don't you see? I'm giving you a gift. Your answers are in that mystery code, too. I tried to tell you that at the lab. All the answers any of us will ever have are written down inside every cell of our bodies. It isn't necessary for you to wander the earth looking for them. I'll find them for you. My colleagues and I will find them all, sooner or later. You can just sit back and relax.''

I was already too relaxed, too low in my chair for common politeness. And my eyes were closing. Then they were closed.

I forced them open and saw Wayne Woodson across the table from me, back from wherever Garrity had sent him to hide. He was leaning into me, his eyes standing out from his contorted face like the eyes of a cartoon hypnotist. I wanted to look around for Wiese, but those eyes wouldn't let me.

''What have you done to Rebecca?'' I demanded.

''What have you done to my daughter?''

''I've saved her,'' I said.

''Do you really believe that? Do you honestly believe that your meddling has ever accomplished any good?''

''Yes.''

''What? Spread a little truth around in a world of untruth? Those are meaningless terms. Have your mysteries ever taught you anything? Have you ever learned a single truth? *The* single truth? If you have, why do you keep on meddling? How many epiphanies does one man need? Is your memory bad? Do you keep finding the answer and forgetting it again?''

He laughed at that, his head back, his beard curling skyward at the tip. ''You go on because you've never found a thing. Not because you turned left when you should have turned right back in college. Learning the truth about your friend Avery just gave you a glimpse of the void. Not your first and not your last. Every time you see it, you shut your eyes to it and stumble on. When